BO AT IDITAROD CREEK

KIRKPATRICK HILL

ILLUSTRATIONS BY LEUYEN PHAM

SQUARE
FISH

HENRY HOLT AND COMPANY

NEW YORK

My thanks to Alfred Miller, who grew up in a town much like Iditarod Creek and who patiently answered all my questions; to my dear daughter-in-law Suzanne Hill, who, unasked, did the Internet research for me; and to Terry Sweetsir, who told me his tooth story so long ago.

SQUARE
FISH

An imprint of Macmillan Publishing Group, LLC
175 Fifth Avenue
New York, NY 10010
mackids.com

Our books may be purchased in bulk for promotional, educational, or business use. Please
contact your local bookseller or the Macmillan Corporate and Premium Sales Department
at (800) 221-7945 ext. 5442 or by e-mail at MacmillanSpecialMarkets@macmillan.com.

Library of Congress Cataloging-in-Publication Data
Hill, Kirkpatrick.
Bo at Iditarod Creek / Kirkpatrick Hill ; illustrated by LeUyen Pham.
pages   cm
Sequel to: Bo at Ballard Creek.
Summary: In 1920s Alaska, when five-year-old Bo and her two adoptive fathers move to
Iditarod Creek to work at a new gold mine, Bo feels homesick until she realizes there is
friendship to be found everywhere—and Iditarod Creek may hold some surprises for her
already unconventional family.
ISBN 978-1-250-07970-1 (paperback) — ISBN 978-1-62779-253-0 (e-book)
1. Alaska—History—1867–1959—Juvenile fiction. [1. Alaska—History—1867–1959—Fiction.
2. Family life—Alaska—Fiction. 3. Adoption—Fiction. 4. Moving, Household—Fiction.]
I. Pham, LeUyen, illustrator. II. Title.
PZ7.H55285Bp 2014   [Fic]—dc23   2014027021

Originally published in the United States by Henry Holt and Company
First Square Fish Edition: 2016
Book designed by April Ward
Square Fish logo designed by Filomena Tuosto

1   3   5   7   9   10   8   6   4   2

AR: 4.9 / LEXILE: 760L

For my accomplished grandchildren:
Meghan, Hayley, Lex and Rowan, Hank,
Ewan, Lewis, Jake, Ian, Aubrey, and Jack.
And for the two I've borrowed—
Max and Eliza.

—K. H.

CONTENTS

CHAPTER ONE: THE PAPAS 1

CHAPTER TWO: THREE RIVERS 9

CHAPTER THREE: GHOST TOWN 22

CHAPTER FOUR: IDITAROD CREEK 38

CHAPTER FIVE: SWEARING 53

CHAPTER SIX: NEW HOUSE 70

CHAPTER SEVEN: BUDDY AND WILL 79

CHAPTER EIGHT: HOUSE WITH THE GREEN ROOF . . . 93

CHAPTER NINE: THE DREDGE 107

CHAPTER TEN: IDITAROD CREEK LADIES 121

CHAPTER ELEVEN: VISITORS 131

CHAPTER TWELVE: TWO KINDS OF WRITING 139

CHAPTER THIRTEEN: THE STRAIGHT LADY 143

CHAPTER FOURTEEN: DOC LARUE 150

CHAPTER FIFTEEN: A BIRTHDAY AND A NAME 158

CHAPTER SIXTEEN: THE DEACON 169

CHAPTER SEVENTEEN: DOUGHNUTS 173

CHAPTER EIGHTEEN: FOURTH OF JULY 178

CHAPTER NINETEEN: AUGUST 193

CHAPTER TWENTY: WINTER COMING 201

CHAPTER TWENTY-ONE: FIRST DAY OF SCHOOL 209

CHAPTER TWENTY-TWO: THE PACKAGE 219

CHAPTER TWENTY-THREE: CHARLIE HOOTCH 226

CHAPTER TWENTY-FOUR: MEETING RENZO 231

CHAPTER TWENTY-FIVE: FOUR MORE 236

CHAPTER TWENTY-SIX: EIGHT CHARLIES 242

CHAPTER TWENTY-SEVEN: THE PIANO BOX 245

CHAPTER TWENTY-EIGHT: BRUISES 252

CHAPTER TWENTY-NINE: QUIET 259

CHAPTER THIRTY: ANOTHER BOY 265

CHAPTER THIRTY-ONE: BACK TO WORK 270

CHAPTER THIRTY-TWO: EERO AND STIG 273

AUTHOR'S NOTE 282

CHAPTER ONE
THE PAPAS

BO'S PAPAS were Jack Jackson and Arvid Ivorsen. She didn't have a mama.

Bo started out with a mama, of course. Everyone does.

Hers was Mean Milly—not a nice motherly sort of person as anyone could tell from her name—but Mean Milly didn't want the job of mama, so she took off. Just before she got on the steamboat headed upriver she marched over to Arvid, who was standing on the riverbank smoking a cigarette, and shoved her baby at him.

A few minutes later Jack came out of the mine cookshack and there was Arvid looking startled, standing on the banks of the Yukon with a baby in his arms, watching the steamboat go away.

Jack could see that Arvid didn't know one thing about newborns because of the way the baby's head was wobbling around. But Jack was an expert on the subject, so naturally they partnered up to take care of Bo.

And that's how Bo came to have no mama and two papas.

SHE WASN'T long out of diapers when she found that it wasn't the usual arrangement. And she could see that hers weren't the usual sort of fathers. People meeting them for the first time would get this look on their faces the way people do when they come up against something out of the ordinary. Trying not to look surprised, trying to pretend they'd seen fathers like that *lots* of times.

For one thing, her papas were so much the same. Both massive, with bulging arm muscles straining the sleeves of their shirts. And very tall. You don't often see *one* man that big, and so two of them together is the kind of thing you can't quite take in for a minute.

Other than that, they were completely different. Arvid had ice blue eyes and straight Swedish hair, getting a little thin on top. He always swore in Swedish.

Jack was black with smoky gray eyes and a soft Southern way of talking. He hardly ever swore.

Bo called them both Papa, which might have gotten confusing, but it didn't.

When Graf came along, the papas hardly blinked. Just added him to the mix.

Explaining about unusual things can get long and complicated, so when someone asked how he and Arvid came to have two kids, Jack would just smile and say it was downright uncanny how he and Arvid were always both there, right on the spot, whenever someone was giving kids away.

ARVID AND JACK had known each other a long time when they got Bo. Arvid came north during the big Klondike gold rush in 1897, and Jack came a few years later along with hordes of other men. That gold rush fizzled out fast, and most of those stampeders, disgusted and broke, couldn't leave fast enough. But some, like Jack and Arvid, stayed—because they liked the mining life and because they liked the country.

Over the next twenty years Jack and Arvid often crossed paths in one mining camp or another, had a game of cards or teamed up to do some blacksmithing. They were both working at the Rampart mine when Bo happened to them.

Right after that, Jack and Arvid went to work at the Ballard Creek Mine up the Koyukuk River. Jack was the camp cook, and Arvid did the blacksmithing. But after they got Graf, the mine ran out of gold, closed down, and the papas had to find another job. They had to leave the place that had been Bo's home for all of her life.

So they were on the way to their new job in a mining camp, which was far away in the Iditarod country. Down two big rivers and up two.

Down was easier because they could just glide along the cold river, using the long pole to steer. Up was harder because they had to travel against the current. Then they might have to use the little three-horsepower gas engine—but not any more than they had to because gas was hard to come by.

Bo and Graf were under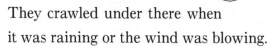
the bow, snuggled into
the billow of down
sleeping bags their
papas kept stored there.
They crawled under there when
it was raining or the wind was blowing.

Bo was trying to teach Graf how to think back-wards. Graf had only belonged to them for a little while, so she wanted him to see how lucky it was that they'd all ended up together.

But thinking backwards took imagination, and she wasn't sure Graf had any.

It was Jack who had taught Bo how to think backwards.

"A lot of little things have to happen first before a big thing can happen. Really tiny things—things no one would pay any attention to—could change someone's life forever," he said.

Like if Arvid hadn't stopped to have a cigarette, Bo wouldn't ever have belonged to the papas. Just a little, little thing like that had turned her life in a completely different direction.

Bo did a lot of thinking backwards. Jack said she

was really good at it, because it was like anything else. If you practice a lot, you improve. But you could get carried away—go backwards on and on, all the way to the beginning of the earth.

You had to know when to stop.

The papas had pulled their yellow slickers on when it started to rain. Jack was hunkered near the bow, reading the water under the brim of his rain hat. Arvid was standing spread-legged for balance, steering the boat with the long pole.

If a wind whipped up and turned the river rough, or if the rain fell so hard they couldn't see anymore, the papas would pull the boat up on the beach, and they'd wait it out.

But it wasn't that bad yet.

It was noisy under the bow, the little waves slap-slapping against the bottom of the boat, the raindrops drumming over their heads on the wood of the bow, so Bo had to talk loudly.

"See, Max always brought the mail in the winter with his dog team and Silver was his lead dog. But Silver got a hurt foot, and Max had to put him in the sled. And he hooked up Frosty to take his place.

But Frosty wasn't as hard-pulling a dog as Silver, so Max was late with the mail."

She paused dramatically. "See, if Max wasn't late, he wouldn't have been behind you and your dad. He would have been *ahead* of you. So he never would have found you in the mail shack. And you would have frozen. And it's all because of Silver's hurt foot!"

Bo thought she had told all this very well, but Graf just gave her a troubled look and didn't say anything.

Bo decided to give up on thinking backwards.

"Do you remember your dad?"

He didn't answer, and she hadn't expected him to. Graf wasn't a big talker.

His dad had died in that mail shack, but Graf never talked about anything that happened to him before they got him. Arvid said maybe he didn't remember, and Jack said maybe he didn't *want* to.

She snuggled down and pulled a sleeping bag up over her. The thrumming rain always made her sleepy.

Suddenly Graf's head popped out of the sleeping bag, a tuft of hair standing straight up.

"He got sick."

Bo nodded, startled.

"He had a fingernail was torn off." Graf pointed to his index finger to show her which one.

"Oh," said Bo, getting that lurch in her stomach that she always got when someone was hurt. "How did that happen?"

Graf gave a little shake of his head. Didn't know.

Bo smiled. Graf had started to open up.

CHAPTER TWO

THREE RIVERS

WHEN THEY LEFT Ballard Creek, the boys from the mine had given them the records and the gramophone from the bunkhouse to keep them company on their trip.

Jack had fixed a place for it on the bow of the boat, tied it down with ropes to keep it steady. When the weather was good and the river was smooth, they played all their favorite songs: "Bye-Bye, Blackbird," "Five Foot Two, Eyes of Blue," "Toot, Toot, Tootsie."

It was a good thing they had their music, because

the first river, the Koyukuk, was a long, lonely river. Five hundred miles, and they hardly saw anyone at all.

"Why aren't there any people?" Bo asked.

"Hard country," was all Arvid said.

But they saw fat porcupines waddling busily along the banks, and moose stripping the new green leaves from the willows. The moose were skinny from the long winter, their thick winter coats shedding off in ragged swatches.

When the moose saw the boat, they'd take fright—roll their eyes, heave their huge bodies back into the undergrowth, and disappear into the dark woods. Bo wished she could pet one.

Down the river they went—one papa minding the boat, reading the water, steering—while the other papa hunkered down in the boat with Bo on one big thigh and Graf on the other. And they'd talk about the things they were seeing.

Lots of trees hung over the river, straight out, barely clinging to the soil with their root toes.

"Look, Papa, those trees crowding behind are meanies. They just shoved and shoved until the front ones fell over," said Bo.

The papas stayed away from the bank when there were trees like that.

"Be bad news to be under one when it falls," Jack said.

Everywhere there were crowds of wild roses and bluebells, and around every bend, ravens high in the spruce trees screamed to warn one another when they saw the boat.

On the sandbars there were strange twisted driftwood shapes, the skeletons of those trees that had been pushed off the bank, and sometimes there were strolling pigeon-toed bears.

Once they saw a big mama bear with five cubs. Five. The littlest was no bigger than a rabbit.

"Likely that mama bear

picked up another sow's cubs for some reason, because look, they're different sizes. Hard to believe it's one litter," Jack said. "I never heard about a bear having so many at one go. Maybe she's just a good-hearted mama bear, taking in strays."

Bo made up a story in her head about how the mama was raising all the orphans, like her and Graf, and she told it to Graf at night when they were tucked into their sleeping bags under the bow of the boat.

She thought how nice it would be to have five children. In Ballard Creek, no one had five kids. Oscar's mama had three, and that was the most anyone had. Bo popped her head out from under the bow.

"Papa, how many children can there be in a family?"

Jack raised his eyebrows and looked at Arvid. "What now?" he said.

Arvid laughed. "Family I knew in Washington had seventeen," he said. Bo looked at him to see if he was serious, then went back under the bow. She was sure Arvid was joking.

BO HAD A LOOSE TOOTH, right in front on the top, in the exact same place Oscar had his first loose tooth. Oscar was Bo's best friend in Ballard Creek. Oscar's tooth fell out, left a wonderful bloody hole, and everyone in Ballard gave him pennies.

Bo wanted to have hers fall out at Ballard Creek as well so she could show everyone, especially Oscar. And get pennies. But it hadn't fallen out.

Her tooth had been loose for weeks, but this time when she prodded it, it didn't pop back up again like it usually did.

"Papa," she said urgently to Jack, "I think it's coming out."

Jack tipped her chin up with one big finger and said, "Yes, ma'am, just hanging on by a thread. Little twist and—"

Out it came.

Bo looked lovingly at the little white tooth in Jack's hand. Then she got a can of tomatoes from the grub box to use for a mirror, and she examined her new hole from every angle in the shiny top of the can.

"I wish I could show
Oscar," she said.

THERE WERE LOTS of
things for Bo and Graf to do
in the boat. They'd stick their
hands in the cold river and
twist them this way and that
to make the patterns in the
water change—braided one way,
braided another, wavy lines sideways, big waves that curled over.

And they could watch the clouds boiling and
shifting into different pictures. Then they'd argue
because they never could agree about what the pictures were.

They made some people out of funny twisted
driftwood branches and played pretend with them
under the bow, out of the sun.

Bo liked to imagine all sorts of adventurous
things with their people, but as soon as she started
with something like, "Pretend there are crocodiles,"
Graf would frown.

"No! I don't want my man to be scared."

So Bo'd have to make her pretend not so danger-ous and exciting.

When they were tired of doing those things, Jack and Arvid told them all the stories they could think of and taught them crazy old songs—"Polly Wolly Doodle," "Keemo Kimo," "Billy Boy."

Jack made a checkerboard from a piece of drift-wood and showed them how to play checkers with black rocks and white rocks for the checkers. Which they didn't play at all by the rules.

ARVID SHOVED THE POLE hard into the river bot-tom, and the boat swerved and came to a stop, grat-ing on sand.

"Time for lunch," Jack said.

Jack jerked his chin at them and threw his thumb over his shoulder. That meant get off into the brush and pee.

Every time they stopped, the papas would make them pee. Even if they didn't have to.

Bo and Graf wore all their winter gear because it was very cold on the river in early summer. So Bo had to struggle with her snowsuit as well as her overalls before she could pull down her panties and then she had to be careful not to pee on everything. And she had to be careful not to get her behind scratched by the evil thornbushes that were everywhere. But it was no problem for Graf. Just a few buttons to undo and that was it.

"It's too bad that girls have such a lot of work to pee, when boys have it so easy," she grumbled.

The papas didn't have anything to say to that, just gave each other one of those looks and grinned.

Graf and Bo were so cramped up in the boat they nearly exploded with energy when the papas pulled off the river for lunch or to camp at night.

They ran and ran up and down the sandbar like wild things, covered themselves with sand, dug

holes with anything handy, and looked for interesting rocks. They wanted to bring the best rocks with them in the boat, but the papas would just raise an eyebrow. No room for rocks, no kind of way.

AFTER MANY LONG DAYS on the Koyukuk, they took a right turn onto the wide, wide Yukon River. Bo and Graf were surprised to see that the Yukon was a completely different color than the Koyukuk. Like coffee with lots of cream.

"Full of silt," Jack said. "And silt is bad news. You'll see when I give you a bath."

It was true about the silt. The water was scratchy on their skins, and there was powdery silt on their clothes after Jack washed them.

But the Yukon wasn't a lonely river. A lot of boats were on the river now that it was nearly clear of ice.

Once they even met a boat with a gramophone like theirs playing on the bow. The sound of the two different kinds of music mixed together for a minute, and the men in the other boat waved and cheered at them as they passed, going the other way.

Here and there were wood camps with hundreds

of cords of firewood stacked on the bank. Bo and Graf had never seen so much wood.

"The sternwheelers stop at these wood camps and the deckhands take all that wood down to the furnace room," Arvid told them. "Got a huge furnace that makes the steam that turns the paddle wheels.

"But you'd never believe how much wood those boats burn up. Can't go far before they got to stop and get another hundred cords," he said. "All along the river here, you'll see big naked places where every tree's been cut for the boats. Makes you wonder."

A big fishwheel, turning slowly, *screek*, *screek*, meant they would come to a fish camp soon. The fishwheels scooped up the fish heading upriver to spawn, hundreds of them.

"Catch a lot more with a fishwheel than a net," Arvid said. "When the Chinamen came north in the gold rush, they showed everyone how they caught fish in China. Started a big fad. Now we got fishwheels on every river in Alaska. Good ideas spread fast."

The papas liked to stop at the wood camps or the fish camps every so often to pass the time of day, hear the news. And buy some smoked fish. Smoked fish was Arvid's favorite thing in the world.

When Jack and Arvid got out of the boat to tie up, people at the camp would stop short for a minute. Surprised. Bo knew that was because they were so big. But they'd have everyone laughing in no time. The papas always joked with everyone.

Some of the children in the camps could speak English, and some spoke only Indian. But Bo and Graf could understand them, and they could understand Bo and Graf.

WHEN THEY TURNED OFF the wide Yukon into the little Innoko River, the air was warmer, and they were glad to take off their snowsuits.

But suddenly there were swarms of mosquitoes. The papas' backs were covered with them, hardly an inch of shirt showing, and Bo and Graf had to wear gloves and rubber boots and button their shirts up tight, even though it was so warm. The mosquitoes' never-ending thin whine—*nnnnnn*—was horrid.

"I wouldn't mind mosquitoes near so much if they didn't make that s*ound*," Arvid complained bitterly.

They kept a coffee can of Buhac burning on the bow, which didn't help much, and they rubbed Bo and Graf with citronella oil, which smelled terrible and gave Graf a rash. They'd suffer it awhile, but then they'd dip their hands in the river and scrub the citronella off their faces. So their faces and hands were swollen with mosquito bites that they scratched until they bled. One day Graf's eyes were almost swollen shut.

"God almighty," said Jack. "Makes me sick to see you chewed up like that."

Bo and Graf had been sleeping in the boat, but now they all slept on the sandbars around a big smoky fire the papas made to keep the mosquitoes off. They kept as close to the smoke as they could, but if the wind shifted, they had to get up and move into the smoke again.

Some miners going down the river gave the papas mosquito netting, and Arvid made head nets for all of them. That was better than citronella, but Bo and Graf didn't like looking at things through the net. It made everything look dark.

They were two weeks on that river, and the mosquitoes were terrible all the way.

"I hate mosquitoes," said Graf, and that was the only time he'd ever given an opinion about anything.

CHAPTER THREE
GHOST TOWN

AFTER THEY'D PASSED the tiny town of Dementi, they left the Innoko River and turned onto the Iditarod River, which twisted and looped and coiled like a crazy thing.

At first it was fun to go around the river bends craning their necks to see what would be there. Once they saw a huge beaver dam in the brush beyond the river. It was so big they could have all lived in it—even the papas.

And once they saw a family of otters happily sliding down the muddy bank, for all the world like a bunch of children. Bo thought they looked like they were laughing.

The otters dove into the water when the boat came near them, and Bo felt bad to spoil the good time they were having.

Jack slowed the boat so they could look at the slick mud slide the otters had made.

Bo had never wanted to do anything as much as she wanted to try that slide.

"Well, you wouldn't scoot down like that, slick as butter on a griddle. It's that silky otter fur makes them slide like that."

Bo nodded. She could see that was true.

But usually there was never anything to see, just another bend coming. Sometimes the river made a sharp hairpin turn, and they'd be going right back the same way they'd just come.

"It's like the ribbon candy Milo has at the store at Christmas," Bo said.

"It's like running in place," Jack said with a disgusted face. "You never seem to get anywhere."

Hundreds of miles of leafy trees stretched beyond the river and crowded around them on the riverbanks. Bo loved the sound they made, shushing and sighing. Noisy trees. The trees around Ballard had been mostly spruce; spruce were quiet trees.

The papas liked that leafy sound too. "Sounds just like the ocean," Arvid said. "Just the way surf sounded washing on the beach when I was a boy." He looked happy remembering that.

The going was slow and tedious, and sometimes they went nearly mad with the sameness of it. They were tired of their records and tired of singing and tired of going around bends and loops and being in the boat. They were tired of mosquitoes. It seemed that they'd been in the boat forever. Even Graf was getting peevish, though he was usually even tempered.

Bo almost couldn't remember Ballard Creek, her head was so full of river and cut banks and sandbars and willows.

When the river turned into treeless tundra country, it finally straightened out. They were all relieved not to be looping back and forth.

And then, out of nowhere, there was a town in front of them on the right bank. A very big town. Bo could hardly believe what she was seeing. After all the weeks of river and sandbars and willows, how could a town just pop up—a town that looked like a picture from a magazine?

"This is where we park the boat," Arvid said. "No more rivers. End of our trip. After we catch the tram to Iditarod Creek, we're done traveling."

They all stared. Streets, more streets than Bo and Graf had ever seen in their lives, more buildings, street after street, building after building.

All empty.

Arvid saw the way they looked. "I know what you're thinking, you two. I heard about this place lots of times, but somehow I never pictured it just like this. Just about the most lonesome-looking thing I ever saw."

Bo squinted intently at the empty streets, looking from building to building, puzzled. "Where are all the people?" she asked finally.

"This is what you call a ghost town." Arvid stood stock-still, looking around at all the buildings.

Jack was staring too. "Lots of them in Alaska," he said, "now the gold rushes are over. Not this big, though. This here is uncommon big." He took his fedora off and fanned his face. "Imagine this place full of people, thousands, come in here on the

stampede, all of them looking to get rich. Built this whole town in a few months."

"Why'd they leave?" Bo asked.

"Same reason we had to leave Ballard. Gold ran out." Jack looked down at Bo and Graf and shook his head. "If there's one thing you can count on not counting on, it's gold," he said.

Old beat-up stern-wheelers sagged into the bank, and splintered waterlogged boards and lumber scraps—bits of old docks and boardwalks—were scattered around the riverfront.

It was quiet, quiet. No birds because there were no trees, just little willows pushing up here and there in the gravel.

The papas tied up the boat, and then they took Bo's and Graf's hands between them and started to walk. They walked up and down the streets, peering into the windows, or the spaces where the windows had been. There were three streets packed with houses and stores, long rotting boardwalks in front of all the buildings, and all the buildings empty.

Some houses were partly torn down so they could see the rooms inside, with scraps of curtains against the windows, broken bits of furniture, wallpaper on the walls. People had lived in those houses, cooked their meals, talked to one another. Empty and silent now.

The stores and businesses had big painted signs on the front, and some of the buildings had tall fronts and short backs. Jack said they built them that way so the building would look like it was two stories, when it was really only one. Bo thought that was very silly, because all you had to do to see that the building wasn't telling the truth was look behind it.

"Tell me the signs," said Bo, and Jack read them out: JOHNSON'S POOL HALL. TOOTSIE'S RESTAURANT. ABE APPLEBAUM'S MERCANTILE. THE IDITAROD CHRONICLE—a newspaper, Jack said.

After that, there were banks, three of them, which the papas had to explain.

"See, you put money in there to be safe, and when you want to spend it, they give it back to you. And maybe if you need some money to build a house or something, they give it to you. Lend it to you. But you have to pay it back."

"Did you put your money in a bank?" she asked. The papas looked at each other and laughed.

"Never had it long enough to put it anywhere," said Arvid.

"Me, I always had the feeling I wanted my money with me all the time, not off somewhere else," said Jack. "I'd be lonesome without it!"

There were two haberdasheries right next door to each other. Bo and Graf tried to say that word but couldn't get it right.

"What does it mean?" Bo asked.

"Place you buy clothes for men," Jack said.

"But why don't they just put up a sign that says clothes for men? Why do they put haber and what else you said?"

Jack and Arvid looked at each other again. "Beats me," said Jack with his eyebrows up.

A barbershop, a little hospital, and a lot of saloons were on the last street.

"I've lost count of the saloons," Jack said.

The biggest one had the biggest sign—IDITAROD

SALOON—printed in fancy red and black letters with curlicues. Bo stopped to admire it. Those letters were so beautiful.

"When I learn to write, I want to write like that," she said. "All fancy."

They carefully lifted open the saloon door because it was hanging on only one hinge. For a minute, they stood by the door and listened to the thick, heavy quiet.

A long table in the middle of the room had a green cloth on it.

"That's a funny table," Bo said.

"It's a pool table," Jack said. "That's a game. Used to be good at this," he said, giving her a smug smile. "Don't see any balls or cues." Jack bent over the table and pretended to hold a long stick. "See, you got to hit the balls into those little pockets."

Bo thought it looked too easy to be a good game.

The green cloth was shredded in places.

"Shrews," said Arvid. "It's their town now." Bo got a picture in her head of busy little shrews bustling up and down the streets, in and out of the stores, shopping.

When they came out of the saloon, they stopped short. They heard hammering.

"Someone still here," said Jack.

They walked toward the sound, and when they came around the corner of a tall half-wrecked building, they saw a skinny man in overalls. He was clawing boards off an upright stud with a crowbar. The nails and the boards squeaked and groaned so loudly that the man didn't hear Jack when he called out.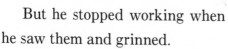

But he stopped working when he saw them and grinned.

"Welcome to Bonanza City," he said, making a funny little bow. He walked up to Jack and Arvid and craned his neck back to look into their faces. "Big guys," he said, almost to himself. Then he shook hands with both of them. "Zeke's my name. Hardy at the hotel said you'd be coming."

The papas told him their names and then Jack said, "Guess you're the wrecking crew."

"Righto. I pull the houses down, take the wood to Iditarod Creek. No trees around here to speak of, so the lumber is much appreciated."

Jack was still staring around him, as if he couldn't take it all in.

"This must be the biggest ghost town in Alaska," he said.

"By far, by far," said Zeke. "Was the biggest town in Alaska after the stampede in 1910. Lasted two years, that's all. Two years. Gold was too deep. And it cost too much to get it out. Then they found gold at Iditarod Creek, just eight miles away." Zeke pointed his thumb over his shoulder to show them where that was.

"Shallow ground there, gold just about popping out of the ground on its own. So everyone in Bonanza City was off and running to get in on it. But that didn't last long. When they brought the dredges to Iditarod Creek, most of those men were out of work again. Dredge takes the place of a hundred men, you know."

"Bedamned," Jack said, shaking his head. "A hundred men."

"Some of the boys went to Nome for the big strikes, some to the Kantishna. Some back home."

Jack and Arvid knew how it was. "Mining life's sure not something you want to depend on," said Arvid.

"Which outfit you working for?" Zeke asked.

"Petrovich," said Arvid.

Zeke smiled. "Good. He's a good one. Wouldn't want to work for Eller's outfit."

"How's that?" asked Jack.

Zeke made a raspy sound in his throat. "His wife runs it, that's why," he said. "A right old battle-ax, her."

The papas grinned at each other. Bo knew she mustn't interrupt grown-ups when they were talking, but when Zeke went to the shed to put his tools away, Bo whispered, "What's a right old battle-ax, and what's a dredge?"

Jack burst out laughing. "You'll see both of them when we get where we're going, I guess. Hold on to your britches until then."

The papas told Bo and Graf that they'd be riding the tram to Iditarod Creek. Trams were really just big wagons that ran on train rails across the tundra.

"And the tram's pulled by horses," Jack said.

Bo looked around wildly. "Where are the horses?"

"Take it easy." Jack laughed. "You'll see them when you see them."

When Zeke came back, Arvid asked, "When's the tram running?"

"Oh, he'll be here soon. I know he was needing to shoe Goldie. That's his best horse," Zeke explained to Bo. "He thinks the sun rises and sets on his Goldie. He's got twelve horses altogether, but Goldie's his favorite."

Across the tundra they could see the wooden rails of the tram, and before long they could see the tram coming closer and closer. Six big horses, hitched by twos, and six flatcars to ride in and carry their freight.

Bo took Graf's hand when the horses got nearer, in case he might be afraid. Which he was.

The tram man was named Charlie.

"There's nine Charlies in Iditarod Creek," he said to Bo. "What do you think about that?"

His name was Charlie Ross, but he said they called him Charlie the Tram.

"The other Charlies is called different things so

you could tell us apart. Little Charlie and Charlie One-Eye—like that," Charlie the Tram explained.

Bo and Graf looked at each other wide-eyed. A one-eyed man!

Charlie smiled down at them. "Want to sit up here on Goldie?" He looked at the papas to see if they'd allow it. "She's good as gold, that's why I call her that."

Jack looked at Bo. "Want to?"

"Yes," she whispered, too pleased to say it out loud. The scow man had never let the children at Ballard Creek near his horses. He said children spooked horses.

Jack scooped Bo up and set her on Goldie's back. Goldie turned her head and looked calmly at Bo. Bo could see she liked children.

"You hold on tight, now," Charlie said.

Graf hid behind Arvid's big leg and peered out. Arvid looked down at him. "You?"

Graf shook his head hard. *No.*

Bo was up high, her head level with Jack's. She gently smoothed the rough hair on Goldie's neck.

"She's so warm, Papa. I wish we could have a horse."

"Used to have plow horses like this down South," said Jack. "Just the smell of a horse puts me in mind of home. But this country's no good for horses. All the horses I ever seen since coming into the country had hard times. Most didn't live long. Died like flies on the Klondike."

"I was on the Klondike," said Charlie. "Break your heart, the lives those horses lived. But my horses got it good. I give them the best of everything, always got six resting while the other six work. I can't abide a man mistreats his animals."

Jack ran his hand over Goldie's rump. "I can see she's well treated," he said to Charlie.

Bo sat on Goldie while the papas and Charlie and Zeke brought their things from the boat and piled them into the open tram cars.

Horses smelled different from anything she'd ever smelled before. And she could feel Goldie's powerful muscles move when she stamped her heavy foot or turned her head.

When Bo talked, Goldie laid her ears back as if she were trying to hear every word.

"Look, Papa, she knows her name."

"Oh, horses is smart," said Charlie the Tram.

The papas pulled the boat into the big shed down by the old dock. Charlie said everyone from Iditarod Creek left their boats there to keep them out of the weather.

Bo felt strange for a moment, seeing the empty boat disappearing into the shed. It had been home for a long time.

When all their things were loaded up and they were ready to go, Jack gave Bo her hat. "Pull down that net if the mosquitoes get bad," he said.

Bo was almost too excited to notice anything, but after a while, she could see that the tundra they were passing over so smoothly was just like the tundra back home in Ballard Creek—humpity tussocks and all the little white flowers, reindeer moss, little baby spruce trees here and there, and far away a row of tall spruce trees edging a creek.

So that was at least one thing that would be the same in their new place—the tundra.

CHAPTER FOUR

IDITAROD CREEK

BEFORE THEY COULD see the town of Iditarod Creek, they began to hear a dreadful rumbling. The closer they got, the louder the noise became, now with piercing high screeks of metal grating and scraping, squeals and roars, growling, slamming, terrible crashing. Bo turned her head to give a horrified look at the papas, so Jack got out of the tram and walked beside her and Goldie.

"That's a dredge, for sure," said Jack. "Never heard one myself, but can't be anything else. Make your blood run cold, if you didn't know what it was, sounds so terrible. It *is* terrible, if you think of it. Like a big monster eating up the earth. And they got four of them. Four dredges around here."

Then suddenly they could see the little town. It was in a narrow valley with low rounded hills all around, but the houses weren't in the hills, and the beautiful tundra was buried in gravel. Arvid tipped his fedora back and shook his head in wonder.

"Will you look at this," Jack said. "Heard about it, but never thought what it would look like."

It was a strange sight. Bo thought the town looked like a bunch of children had been playing with toy houses and had just put them down any old way. All the houses and stores and other buildings were laid out all higglety-pigglety on vast stretches of rough gravel. The gravel—called tailings—was what was left after the gold had been taken out of the rocks.

And nowhere a tree or a bush. Just heaps of gravel and scattered buildings on the tailings. No beaten paths between the houses like in Ballard. Just tailing piles.

"Where are the trees?" Bo asked.

"Under these tailing piles, I guess," said Jack.

"Everything covered with gravel. Never saw so much gravel in my life."

Bo gave Jack a sorrowful look. "No tundra," she said.

When the six good horses stopped at their barn, Jack and Arvid unloaded their freight and carried it into the barn. Charlie the Tram said they could pick up their boxes the next day when they found a place to live. Then they set out for the hotel.

A few men stopped on the way to say hello to them, but it wasn't like Ballard Creek, where everyone in town came to meet the scow.

"Zeke said five hundred people live around here, counting all the mining camps," said Arvid. "So they're not like people at Ballard Creek, crowding around, happy to see a new face."

"How many people is five hundred?" said Bo, who had a problem with big numbers.

"About five times more than Ballard Creek," said Arvid.

"Oh," said Bo, looking blank.

"Yep, been a long time since I was in a place with so many people," said Arvid. "It does take you back a bit."

People on the boardwalks, going in and out of stores, and she didn't know a single one of them. It gave her a strange feeling, and she held Jack's hand tighter. Graf looked as if he felt the same way, so Arvid hoisted him up and carried him the rest of the way to the hotel.

The terrible noise of the dredge never stopped. "Sounds like a never-ending train wreck," Arvid muttered.

Then they saw something so strange they all stopped still.

Along the top of the gravel pile came a big Caterpillar bulldozer. A Cat.

It was pulling a house behind it on a big skid called a go-devil. A whole house, painted yellow, with a tar paper roof and even curtains at the windows. There was a little girl leaning out of the window on one side of the house. And she was waving at them!

"Look at me!" she shouted.

Bo and Graf looked openmouthed at their papas. Jack's eyes went wide. "Beats *me* what she's doing there," he said.

"Don't look safe to me," said Arvid.

"I didn't know houses could move," Bo said.

"Not a thing you'll see very often," said Jack. "Except here. Here I'm told they move houses all the time."

Bo stared at the house inching its way along behind the Cat. The little girl had left the window and was waving at people from a window on the other side.

"Why, Papa? Why do they move them?"

"These houses are sitting on the gold, that's why. When the dredges get finished digging up the gold in one place, they have to turn around and go dig up the ground someplace else. And sometimes that someplace else is under the houses, so the houses have to move."

"Do they move every day?"

"No, but often enough," said Jack.

"Will we live in a house that has to move?"

"Not if I can help it," said Jack grimly.

Some other men stopped to watch the house. They introduced themselves to the papas and then turned and called out rude things to the man who was driving the bulldozer.

"God almighty, Dave, can't you get up a better head of steam than that?" and "Going to be snowing at that rate before you get it moved!"

"That's the third time they moved that house," one man told Jack.

Jack looked amazed. "You wouldn't think a house could stand that treatment more than once."

"Oh, it takes its toll all right. Porch goes back on all crooked, or the house gets out of plumb, trim falls off, that kind of thing. Never quite the same once they're moved, but near every building you see here's been moved once, and a lot of them more than once. You get used to it. My old place is going next." He pointed off in the distance. "Picked a place right next to Frenchie's there, down at the end of that tailing pile."

"You can just pick a new place for your house?"

"Oh, got to get permission from the mine owner, of course, but they're not fussy."

"How come people don't put their houses up on the hills where they won't have to move?"

"Couldn't get water up there, could they? Everyone in town has well water now. Move to the hills, and they'd have to go back to hauling water from the creek or melting snow in the winter. They don't care much where they live long as they got a water pump in the house."

Bo tugged at his shirt. "The little girl, Papa."

Arvid looked down at her. "This is Bo, and she wants to know about the little girl in the house," Arvid said.

"Oh, that's Edna. Spoiled rotten. Does what she wants, whenever she wants. That's Edna for you!"

"I'd tan her hide, was she mine," said the other man.

Arvid was staring at the moving house. "I'd be in a cold sweat, was I pulling that house," he said.

They watched the house and the little waving girl for a minute. The men were so friendly, with happy faces, that Bo began to feel better about Iditarod Creek. And one of the men had hair coming out of his ears in an interesting way.

"Well," said Jack, "we need to get the kids settled, get a good meal in them first thing. Could you point us to the hotel?"

The men told them they couldn't miss it, next street over, tell Hardy we sent you, and they went off laughing.

The hotel was just where the men had said it would be. It was a two-story building—a real one, not just a pretend one like the ones in the ghost town.

A big sign was painted on the front between the upstairs windows: INTERNATIONAL HOTEL. Bo smiled happily. Those letters were as tall as she was.

They all stood on the boardwalk outside the hotel and looked at the notice pinned by the open front door. BREAKFAST SERVED 6 TO 12, LUNCH SERVED 12 TO 1:30, AND DINNER 6 TO 7:30.

"Made it for breakfast," said Arvid, looking pleased.

A man with a dirty apron around his middle and a dish towel over his shoulder came to the door and shook hands with Jack and then Arvid. He was so short he had to tip his head back to look up into their faces.

Then he squatted and shook hands with Graf and Bo. It didn't happen very often that people got down low to talk to them. Bo liked that because it was hard to look up all the time and just see under people's chins when they were talking. She liked this Hardy.

"Just off the tram, eh? Got some nice empty rooms for you," he said. "And got breakfast warming in the oven. You like mush? Ham and eggs?"

He stood up and looked at the papas. "Working for Petrovich, right?" he said. Jack nodded. "He's over at Olnes Creek right now, had coffee here before he left. Said you'd be coming along soon, your bunch. He'll be back in no time."

Hardy jerked his head at Bo and Graf. "Guess you won't be living in the bunkhouse with this crew. He's got some houses he rents out this side of the creek. Probably settle you in there."

He winked at Bo and Graf. "Kids in town'll be

glad to have some fresh blood," he said. Bo slid her eyes at Graf to see if he was worried about the blood business.

Hardy pointed them to a long table in the back of the hotel, which was already set with thick plates and mugs.

"Breakfast in a jiffy," he said.

Hardy brought the coffeepot from the big cookstove at the back of the room and poured coffee for Jack and Arvid. He pushed a can of milk and a big bowl of sugar across the table to them.

"Been wanting a good cup of coffee," Jack said. But Bo could tell that after he took a sip, he didn't think it was a good cup because he put milk and sugar in it, which is what he always said could make bad coffee taste better.

Some men from town came into the hotel and crowded around Jack and Arvid, shaking hands, and some of them helped themselves to coffee from the pot on the stove and sat down with them.

Jack and Arvid had to tell where they'd come

from, and why the Ballard Creek mine folded, and what kind of boat they had and if the engine had silted up on the Yukon. The men joked about working for Petrovich, who they said was a wild man. Bo looked quickly at Jack and Arvid when they said this.

"Done that before," said Arvid. Bo reminded herself to ask Arvid about the time he'd worked for a wild man.

The men told them there were four big dredge mines around Iditarod Creek: Petrovich's, Eller's, the Kilbourne, and furthest away, the Willard dredge. And there was one sort of medium kind of mine, Donal Sather's, which didn't have a dredge but had a Cat and a big digger. All the mines were working twenty-four hours a day, seven days a week, because summer was very short.

While the men were talking, Bo and Graf tipped back their heads to look at the strange lamp in the middle of the ceiling.

Arvid smiled when he saw what they were looking at. "That's an electric lamp. Don't need coal oil for those lamps. You don't do nothing to the lamps. The light just comes down the wires."

Bo and Graf looked at Arvid suspiciously. "I'll show you!" he said. He stood up and put his hand on a chain hanging down from the lamp. "Watch closely!" he said and pulled the chain. The lamp turned on.

"See?" He pulled the chain again and the light turned off. Bo and Graf looked at each other, astonished.

All the men at the table laughed at Bo and Graf. "Same way I felt first time I ever saw electric light," one of them said.

BO HAD THOUGHT a hotel would be something different than a roadhouse, but it wasn't. It was just like the roadhouse in Ballard, really. Just a little bigger. Sleeping rooms were upstairs, and downstairs there was a big table where everyone ate and a lot of little tables and chairs where people could play cards. Bo saw that one table had piles of worn-out magazines. She nudged Graf and pointed. They both loved magazines.

There was a big gramophone, almost like the one Milo had in the roadhouse at Ballard Creek. Bo looked to see what records the hotel had. She couldn't read, but she could tell that some of them were the records they'd had in Ballard.

Over the long bar was a big mirror just like the one in Ballard, just like the one in Bonanza City. Bo was about to ask Hardy why bars always had mirrors when she saw that a lot of framed pictures were hanging up on one side of the mirror. Pictures of fancy-looking families. All the women were wearing big hats.

"Who are those people all dressed up?" asked Bo.

Hardy walked over to the wall with the pictures and tapped the first one with his finger.

"They all mined around here. Took those pictures just before they left Iditarod Creek in the fall, all of them going home for the winter, going Outside. That's Ray Dunfey, his wife and kids." He touched the next picture. "And this here's Clyde and his family, and his two brothers who mined with him.

"And this here's the Mason crew, from over the

hill. They all died on the *Sophia*," said Hardy. "Before you was born. They caught the last boat to Juneau, and that boat they was on got in trouble, and they all drowned. Fifteen of them from here, good people."

"There's *children*," said Bo. She was sure the hotel man didn't mean they'd all died. Not the children.

"Right. That's Micky, right smart little guy, and his sister, Emilia, and that's Jambo, they called him, just twelve, and Carla, belonged to those people on the end. 'Bout broke our hearts here in Iditarod Creek."

Bo stared at the picture. Those children *had* died.

"Three hundred fifty-five people died on that boat, most of them from the mining camps around Alaska, going out for the winter." Hardy unrolled his sleeves, then rolled them back up very carefully. "Twelve years ago," he said. "In 1918." Hardy stood still, looking at the pictures, and then he said, "They never even heard that the war ended." He walked back to the sink and began to wash the beer mugs again.

Bo's throat was tight. Those happy people died right after the picture was taken. All of them together. And the children never got any older.

"There was a dog," said Hardy over his shoulder. "Swam to shore. Only one that lived."

Hardy came back to the bar to stack the beer mugs he'd been drying. He pointed to another picture he had pinned up. "This here is the way the town looked at first," said Hardy. "Used to be laid out real neat, like an Outside town. Before the dredges ripped it up."

All the pretty little houses in the picture were sitting neatly on nice straight streets, and there were grass and flowers in the yards. And trees. Now the houses seemed all tumbled around, set down any which way and looking pretty bedraggled. And there certainly weren't any trees or flowers anymore. Bo couldn't believe it was the same town.

Iditarod Creek was not an ordinary place.

CHAPTER FIVE

SWEARING

TWO SKINNY BOYS, bigger than Bo, were lurking about the hotel door, peeking in at them. They looked a lot alike, with straight brown hair falling in their eyes.

Bo was so happy to see someone near her own age it never occurred to her to be shy. She took Graf by the hand and walked to the door.

"I'm Bo, and this is Grafton," she said. "He's my new brother."

"He don't look that new to me," said the biggest boy in a puzzled kind of way.

"I just got him a little while ago," said Bo.

The boy looked at her intently as if he expected her to say more, but when she didn't, he said, "This here is my brother Leroy, and I'm Will."

Leroy gave Will a cross look.

"No one calls me Leroy, which is a stupid name," he told them indignantly. "Our pa told me that's because my ma said it was her turn to name a baby. And she picked a sissy name."

"Leroy," said Bo slowly, trying it out.

"*Is* sissy," growled Graf. Bo looked at him, shocked. It was the second time that Graf had given his opinion about something. She gave his hand a tiny shake to remind him not to say just anything that popped into his head.

"What do they call you?" asked Bo.

"My pa calls me Buddy, and so does everyone else. Except Ma."

"That's like me," said Bo. "I have a real name— that's Marta—but everyone calls me Bo."

Graf looked at her so sharply that Bo remembered no one had ever told him that she had another name besides Bo.

The boys kept looking through the door at the papas.

"Wow," Will breathed, "they're really big."

"Yeah," said Buddy.

He turned to Bo, his face full of admiration. "Is that one your father?" he asked, pointing to Arvid.

"We have two fathers and no mother," said Bo. The two boys blinked at her, their faces still.

The boys were silent for a moment and then Buddy said, "That's good. If you had two mothers, that could have been bad. Because mothers are the most bossiest ones."

Bo thought about the mothers she knew in Ballard Creek, and she thought it was the fathers who were bossiest there. But she didn't want to disagree with the boy.

"Want to come and play with us?" Will said.

"I'll ask," said Bo.

Arvid was sitting at the end of the table, so she got up on her tiptoes to whisper in his ear. Arvid looked at the boys in the doorway and then gave Bo a worried look.

"Maybe later, Bo," he said. "We need to get settled here. Find out what's what. Maybe you and the boys could play outside the hotel here for a bit, but don't leave. Stay on the boardwalk. Okay? Lots we have to do yet."

Buddy and Will and Bo and Graf sat on the boardwalk with their legs dangling down.

"Do you know the girl in the house that was moving?" asked Bo.

"Oh, that's Edna," said Buddy. "She said she was going to stay in the house when they moved it, and her ma said no, she wasn't going to do no such thing, but Edna always does what she wants, so she hid inside and her ma didn't see."

Will and Buddy smiled at each other in a pleased sort of way, so Bo could tell they liked it that Edna didn't listen to her ma. They didn't seem to have a good idea about any kind of mothers, really.

"How many kids live here?" Bo asked.

"Hardly any," said Will. "Me and Buddy and Edna, and she's only here in the summer because her folks leave in the fall after cleanup. And there's a new kid, lives out the Willard dredge. We never seen him, though. So that's four kids, and now you two."

Bo looked disbelieving. "That man at the ghost

town, that Zeke, he said there were five hundred people around Iditarod Creek."

"Yeah, but they're all men, mostly. It's all mining camps here."

"Where's the school?"

"Not enough kids for a school," said Buddy. "We told you, just us and Edna and that new kid."

"You don't go to school?"

"Oh, we have school, all right. Our ma teaches us. Calvert courses."

"What's that?" Bo asked.

"Don't you know about Calvert courses?" Will looked at her with eyebrows raised. "See, how it works is Calvert sends the lessons from way back East and then you do the lessons, and your ma sends them back East to get a grade, and you keep doing that until you're finished for the year. I'm in the fifth grade, and Buddy's in the fourth. What grade are you in?"

"I'm supposed to be in first this year," said Bo. "I didn't know there wouldn't be a school." She looked sadly down at her feet dangling over the edge of the boardwalk. "School was nice in Ballard Creek.

There was Miss Sylvia and all the big kids, and even some of the grown-ups went, even a grandma, and there was singing, and they did a play for Christmas. And there was a paper all around the wall with the ABCs in printing and in that curly kind of writing."

"That's cursive," said Will. "I'm learning it this year, Ma said. I never did even get good at printing yet, though. Ma says I don't write no better than a hottentot."

"What's a hottentot?"

"I don't know. Someone who's no good at printing."

Buddy had been thinking about what Bo said.

"How come a grandma was going to school?"

"Not just a grandma, there was a father too. There wasn't any school when they were little, so they were going now."

"Whoa," said Buddy. "That's crazy."

"Maybe I'll have to go to school when I'm a grandma if there's no school here," Bo said gloomily.

Will pointed to a house on the edge of town that looked fancier than the other houses. "That's the Eller house."

"It's very tall," Bo said. "Taller than the roadhouse in Ballard Creek. The roadhouse had an upstairs, but it wasn't that tall."

"Got three stories, that house," said Will. "Eller's got to have the biggest and fanciest of everything. To keep his wife happy. He's the boss of the dredge across the hills over there. It's the biggest outfit around here. He has a hundred men working there."

"It's not the dredge your papas will be working on," Buddy said. "My pa said they're working for Petrovich. Different outfit. But our pa works for Eller."

"House's got three stories so Miz Eller can watch us," Will said.

"She watches you?" said Bo.

"Not just us, she watches everyone. She's got big binoculars. See that window up on the top? That's where she likes to spy on us. She'll be watching us right now, to see who come to town. Guess she'll get an eyeful this time—never seen nothing like you bunch."

Buddy and Will smiled at each other, thinking about that. "She mostly watches the boys who work for Eller. And if they do something she doesn't like, she tells her husband."

Bo was bewildered. "Tells him what?"

"Well, like if one of Eller's men was drinking and got the blind staggers or something, she'll tell Eller to fire him. And the boys don't want to get fired, especially in the middle of the mining season, because all the jobs would be taken. So they try to keep on her good side. Ma's always scared Pa will get fired because he argues with Eller sometimes."

Buddy was trying to get a word in. "And see, if anyone visits across the creek, she tells him."

"She doesn't like people visiting?"

"Well, she doesn't like them visiting the good-time girls. And see, there's no trees or bushes or nothing, so no one can't go anywhere without Miz Eller seeing them."

"And, boy," Will said, "she sees everything. Like Ma is scared if she keeps her washing on the line too long, Miz Eller will say she's being lazy or something. And she tells Ma if she sees us doing something she don't like.

"Once she told Ma when we was making this little net across the creek, and she said it wasn't healthy for children to play in the cold creek water and that Ma should keep better control of her children. We couldn't go to the creek for the longest time until Ma kind of forgot about it."

"Oh," said Bo. "*That's* a right old battle-ax!"

Will and Buddy laughed so delightedly that Bo felt uncomfortable. "Well, that's what Zeke, at Bonanza City, said. A right old battle-ax. Eller's wife."

"Oh yeah," said Will, still grinning madly. "Zeke's got *that* right!"

Buddy jumped up. "Let's go see how far Edna got in her house!"

Bo really wanted to watch the house moving. But Graf shook his head at her and then she remembered what Arvid had said.

"Oh, we can't. Papa said to stay right here because we got to find a place to live and all." She looked wistfully down the street. "Are they going to be moving more houses?"

"That's the last one. They already moved five houses last month. See that one over there with the black door? That's ours. Moved it last week. When they get all the houses moved, they'll start thawing the tailings. And then when that's done, they'll move the dredge over here and start eating up the tailing piles."

"At Ballard Creek, no one ever bothered the tailing piles," said Bo.

"Lots of gold under those tailings—that's what they said when they drilled. They said the last dredge didn't dig deep enough."

"Did you feel bad to have your house moved?"

"Nah, we had it moved before when we lived way down there." Will pointed down the river where they could hear the dragline clanking away.

"See, they tell people they got ten days to move to someplace else on the tailing piles. And then, like us, we got the house jacked up and on the go-devil, and Jason pulled it with the Cat to the new place. And then our dad put down a well and stuck our old pump on it and ran the electric lines to the house, and it's all finished."

It was ordinary to Will and Buddy, Bo thought. They sat back down on the boardwalk and dangled some more.

"So how come you got two fathers?" asked Will. Bo felt impatient having to explain, but then she thought that having two fathers was ordinary to her, but not to Will and Buddy. The way it was ordinary for them to move houses.

"Well, me and Graf didn't have any relatives. Graf's dad died, and my mama took off like a turtle."

"Like a turtle?" said Will, with an astonished stare.

"Jack says where he comes from, the mama turtles just lay their eggs and take off."

"Oh," said Will. "We saw that before. Suzie's mama just up and left. Left her with her dad, and then he took Suzie Outside to live with her grandma."

"Well, see," said Bo, "my mama was going to take off, so she gave me to Arvid when he was just minding his own business, smoking a cigarette. And then Jack had to help Arvid, because Arvid didn't know spit about babies. And that made two papas, Arvid and Jack."

"Didn't you have no grandma?"

"No," said Bo. "Didn't have anything. That's why Jack and Arvid took me. And because they didn't want to leave me with the nuns."

"What's nuns?" asked Buddy.

Bo pulled her shoulders up to show that she didn't really know. "Some kind of church people. And Graf didn't have anyone to take him, so his auntie said send him to the nuns, but Jack and Arvid didn't want to do that either. So we got to keep him. And so now I have a brother, and he has a sister, and we have two papas."

Will and Buddy looked respectfully at Bo and Graf.

"Jeez, that's pretty good. Lucky for you." The boys were silent for a minute, thinking.

"Look to be easy-going, your papas," said Will.

Bo wasn't sure what easygoing meant.

"Well, good-natured. Like maybe they don't yell a lot."

Bo and Graf smiled at each other.

"No, they don't yell at us, not mad yell. Jack always rolls his eyes and says 'what next?' if we do something we shouldn't." She could see the boys weren't impressed with that, so she bragged, "But Arvid, he swears in Swedish when he gets riled."

"Wow," said Will. "Wow."

"Swear some Swedish," said Buddy.

Bo was proud to do it. She wished she knew a lot of swearing in Swedish, but Arvid just used the same few words over and over.

"*Vad i helvete*," she said. She put her chin down and tried to swear with a deep, growly voice, kind of loud, like Arvid.

Will and Buddy looked at her, awestruck.

"*Dra åt helvete!*" she shouted.

The boys pressed closer to her.

"*Jävlar! Jävlar!*" she snarled. "That's what you say when you hurt yourself," she explained. "*Jävlar!*" She thought a moment. "*Skit! Skit, skit, skit!*"

She wiped her hands on the front of her overalls.

"That's about it," she said.

"Swearing sounds really, really good in Swedish," Buddy said fervently.

"Could you teach us?" Will asked.

"Sure," said Bo. "But your ma might not like it."

"Shoot, we're not going to swear around Ma. Not in any kind of language. She'd take the hide off us."

"And besides," Buddy said, "she don't know any Swedish."

"Graf and I can swear in Eskimo, too," said Bo. Buddy and Will stared at her.

"Go on," Will said, as if he didn't believe her. Bo could swear a lot more words in Eskimo than she could in Swedish, so she started in.

Then she nodded encouragingly at Graf. "He can, too," she said. "Go on, Graf."

So Graf and Bo swore all the Eskimo swear words they knew. Graf had this funny voice, all growly and rough, and his swear words were the toughest sounding.

"Do it again," the boys begged. Will and Buddy cheered each new word, pounded their knees when there was an especially good one, grinned with delight over the really long ones. When Bo and Graf had said all the Eskimo swear words they knew in as many different ways as they could think of, Will leaned weakly back against the hotel wall. He sighed happily.

"That's the best swearing yet," he said. "Sounds really, really worser in Eskimo. Teach us that long one."

Bo tried, but the boys couldn't make the wet scraggly sounds in their throats at all. So Bo said they should learn the Swedish swearing first because it was easier; you just had to kind of sing it.

Will and Buddy carefully copied Bo, watching her lips.

"*Skit, skit, skit!*" they said, quite well.

It was just then that Arvid came out to get them and when he heard the word they were practicing, he stopped short.

"*Vad i helvete?*" he roared, which made Will and Buddy smile happily.

"Bo! What the . . . Where'd you learn those words?"

Bo blinked. "You're the only one I know speaks Swede, Papa."

"Christ almighty, you're the—" Arvid's face turned very red. "You can't say those words around here." He looked to see if anyone had been listening. "Might be some Swedes—you don't know."

"Well, Papa, they wanted to learn. I was just teaching them."

Arvid looked helpless.

"Don't worry, mister," said Will. "We won't tell no one. Heck, we never tell no one nothing. Guess we know better than that."

Arvid groaned, snatched Graf up off the boardwalk and grabbed Bo's hand.

"Come on, Bo, Graf. We're going to send a wire to Ballard Creek. Let 'em know we got here safe. Gotta find the Signal Corps building."

Will and Buddy jumped to their feet. "We'll take you!" Arvid made a face like he didn't want the boys to show him anything, but they were already scampering ahead.

Bo didn't think Arvid liked their new friends much.

Bo and Graf and Arvid and the boys walked

past the houses scattered every which way on the old tailing piles.

"There's the Signal Corps building," said Buddy, pointing. Then he nodded to a pile of charred lumber. "And that's where they had a big fire before we were born, killed somebody. Guy got drunk and set the house on fire." Then he showed them a little house set crookedly on the tailing piles. "That's the bootleg shack," he said.

Arvid raised one eyebrow at Buddy. "Not much you kids don't know, is there?"

"No, mister," said Buddy.

Arvid made his frowning-thinking face and then he stopped short, grinned his biggest grin, and chuckled.

"Guess I was just the same," he said.

He bent down and put his hand out to Buddy. "Name's Arvid," he said. He shook Will's hand next. "Pleasure to meet you boys," said Arvid.

As he started to walk off toward the Signal Corps building, Arvid called to the boys over his shoulder, "My grandfather could swear for two minutes straight without ever repeating himself."

So that was all right, thought Bo.

CHAPTER SIX

NEW HOUSE

THE NEXT MORNING, when Hardy brought their breakfast, Bo could tell right away that it wasn't like one of Jack's breakfasts. The sausages were burnt and cold, sitting in a little puddle of grease, and the hotcakes were dried out and pale.

She could see by the looks on Jack's and Arvid's faces that they agreed.

Of course, none of them would say anything rude about someone else's cooking. But when Hardy went back to the kitchen to get some more coffee, Arvid mumbled, "Be glad to be eating your cooking again, Jack."

"That's how it is," said Jack. "Don't miss the water till the well runs dry."

Petrovich would rent them one of the houses he kept for his men who didn't live in the camp bunkhouse. Any of his workers who didn't live at the camp got three extra dollars a day. Jack said that was a good deal because they for sure didn't want to live that near the dredge, which clanked and roared day and night.

"Need to get a rest from that when we're off shift," he said. Bo didn't know how he was going to get a rest, because you could hear the Petrovich dredge all over town. But she thought it must be worse to be living right next to it.

After breakfast at the hotel, they borrowed a big wagon from Hardy and moved all their things from Charlie the Tram's barn into their new house.

There was another house not far away from theirs. It had a green roof—such a beautiful green, such a lovely color in the midst of all those gray, drab, treeless tailings. Bo wished someone would come out the door of that house so she could wave at them. She knew she would like people with a roof like that.

Their own house didn't have a pretty roof, but it had electricity and a pump in the kitchen so they didn't need to haul water from the creek.

But of course it needed a lot of scrubbing from Jack's point of view. Jack was a very clean person. What Arvid called crazy-clean.

Bo and Graf had a wonderful time yanking the chains that turned the lightbulbs on and off. When they were tired of that miracle, they pumped water, leaning on the pump handle and swinging down to bring a gush of water from the mouth of the pump. Before long, they were drenched. They filled so many buckets that Jack hollered at them to stop.

"Will it run out, Papa?"

"Guess not, but you'll for sure wear out the pump at this rate!"

There were four rooms and a narrow closet in their new house. The doorway to Bo and Graf's room was covered with a long faded curtain. The other bedroom had the only wooden door that closed, so they all said Arvid had to sleep there because he snored so awful.

"You'll wish you had my snoring instead of that clang-clang-god-rotted dredge noise," said Arvid. Jack looked grim.

"Never thought I'd hear something worse than your snoring, but I have now," Jack said. "I do most sincerely hate the sound of that damn dredge." The look on Jack's face was so cross, Bo and Graf burst out laughing.

Jack would sleep in the little closet. He got a cot from Hardy's hotel, and it was a tight fit. But Jack said he'd slept in lots of worse places, and he'd like it just fine.

The house had some tired, worn-out furniture: a big chest of drawers in the kitchen, a bed and a wooden chair in Arvid's room, two beds for Bo and Graf, and in the living room a long couch which bulged in odd places.

Graf and Bo had never seen a couch before.

"What's that called?" Bo asked.

"A couch," said Arvid.

"A divan," said Jack. The papas looked coolly at each other, and Jack took a quarter out of his pants pocket. "Heads," he said, and flipped the coin up in the air.

Arvid caught it, slapped it on his wrist, looked at it, and said, "Ha!"

They both looked at Bo and Graf and said together, "Couch."

Now that that was settled, Bo and Graf immediately wanted to jump on it. But Arvid said stop because that couch had already been abused and didn't need any more.

A fat stuffed chair sat next to the couch, and Arvid shook his head at them. "Not the chair, neither," he said, in case they were thinking of jumping on that.

The kitchen was the biggest room, but it had a dinky little table instead of that long stretch of table they'd had in the cookshack at Ballard. They all looked at it bleakly.

Twenty people could sit around the table at Ballard. That table had been where Jack rolled out his piecrusts and where Bo drew with her crayons and made houses out of matchboxes. That table had been the center of their lives at Ballard. This sorry little table with wobbly legs and just four chairs made Bo's heart squeeze up with homesickness.

"Don't worry," said Jack, patting her shoulder. "We'll throw together a new table in no time."

Bo looked up at them hopefully. "Big as our old one?"

Jack and Arvid both swept a look down the room, measuring it with their eyes. "Maybe bigger," Arvid said. Bo and Graf looked at each other and smiled. The papas could fix anything.

Bo and Graf helped Jack clean while Arvid went out with Charlie the Tram's wagon to get things they needed at the store. He came back with boards to make a longer table.

"Look, you two," he said. "These are planks Zeke pulled off some old house at Bonanza City. Don't I just wish they could talk."

Graf helped Arvid with the new tabletop, and Bo bustled around doing what Jack told her to. He got on his hands and knees and scrubbed the cracked linoleum with a big brush, while Bo did the windows. Jack gave them another swipe with a clean cloth when she'd finished, and then the windows were shining.

After Jack washed the living room walls, he planed the rough edges off the outhouse seats. "Don't want any splinters in your behinds," he said.

Then he made the beds with their old quilts and flannel sheets and pillows. Bo unpacked Graf's red velvet bear and her much shabbier bear, set them tenderly on the beds, one on each pillow, and patted them lovingly.

Jack smiled down at Bo. "Feels like home now, with your bears talking to each other," he said.

Buddy and Will knocked on the screen door to see if Graf and Bo could come out. Bo said they were too busy, but when the boys turned to go, they stopped and looked at the couch.

"Got a davenport, huh?" Buddy said approvingly. Bo and Graf gave each other a look. Another name for it.

While Jack was settling the little house to his strict standards, Arvid and Graf finished the tabletop.

Jack spread the table with their old flowered oilcloth.

"Nine feet this table is. Almost as long as our old one. Perfect. Can do just about anything on this table."

When they finally sat down to eat at the new table, which Bo and Graf had set with their old plates and cups, Jack looked well pleased. He liked it when everything was orderly.

CHAPTER SEVEN

BUDDY AND WILL

BO AND GRAF were helping Jack put away the breakfast dishes when they heard feet pounding on the path to their door. Bo snatched the door open, and there was Buddy getting ready to knock, with Will behind dancing impatiently up and down on the path.

"Can you come out?"

They'd nearly finished settling in, so the papas said they didn't need any more help.

"Go have some fun," Arvid told them. "You've been slaving away for days."

While Bo looked for Graf's lace-up boots behind the door, Jack wiped his hands and asked the boys if they wanted a leftover biscuit and they did. Will took two.

Bo laced Graf's knee-high leather boots to save time. He could do it himself, but they were in a hurry, and hurry wasn't a thing Graf was good at.

When Graf's boots were laced, they all ran off across the tailings.

First Buddy and Will showed them the dirt airstrip at the edge of town. Buddy showed them what looked like a long hat with a pointy end attached to a tall pole.

"That's the wind sock," he said. "The pilot could look at that and tell which way the wind is blowing. Got to know that when you're landing planes."

"You know a lot about planes," said Bo admiringly.

"That's because we got a job with the mail plane. Chuck—he's the pilot—wires Sherwin when he's coming and then we go tell Charlie the Tram, because he's got to pick up the mail and take it to the post office, and then we go to Hardy and get Chuck's lunch. We make a lot of money—five cents a trip."

After that, Buddy and Will showed them the jailhouse, which didn't have any prisoners, and took them down to the creek to catch guppies.

They all squatted by the creek and stared at the water. "We haven't got anything to catch a guppy with if we see one," Bo pointed out.

"How bears fish," said Will, "is they just scoop it out of the water and onto the bank."

They all stared at the water some more. "Hardly any guppies in here anyway," said Buddy.

"On our way here, we saw a mama bear with five babies," said Bo. "Black bear." Will and Buddy looked astounded, as they often did at the things Bo told them.

"How can that be?" asked Buddy.

"Well, our papas didn't think they were all her babies because they were different sizes. Littlest one wasn't any bigger than a rabbit," she said.

"Wow, I'd like to have seen that," said Will.

Bo thought of something even more amazing to tell them.

"We have this friend in Ballard Creek, that's Olaf," said Bo. "He has a dog and a raven and a weasel and a porcupine and a ptarmigan. They all live with him and never fight."

Will looked at her with one eyebrow raised. "Go on," he said. "No way a weasel's going to live peaceful with all of them. Meanest animals ever, weasels."

"Except wolverines," said Buddy.

"Olaf's weasel isn't mean," said Bo, stung by any criticism of Olaf's animals. "I saw them *lots* of times. They're all friends."

Buddy and Will just looked at each other. "Hmm," said Buddy.

They didn't believe her, Bo could tell.

Will jumped up. "Let's take them to see Maggie!"

"Who's Maggie?"

"She runs the post office," Buddy said. "And she's really skookum," he said, flexing his arm like a prizefighter to show them how strong Maggie was. "Pa says she's solid muscle. She hustles all the big freight boxes like they was nothing."

"She's Athabascan," said Will. "And Frenchie, her husband, he's a Canuck. He works at Sather's mine."

Bo didn't know what any of those things were, but she'd ask the papas later.

"Could we visit the girl who rode in the house?" Bo asked.

"Nah. Edna lives at her pa's mining camp in the summer." Will pointed at the far hills. "A long way away. You'll see her when she comes to town next."

"Oh," said Bo, disappointed.

BO AND GRAF were almost struck dumb by Maggie. Not only was she thick and strong looking, she had a silver tooth that flashed in the sunlight.

She beamed at Bo and Graf. "Frenchie already knows your papas," she said. "Met them at the store."

The post office was just a little house on skids so it could be moved whenever it had to be. There were two rooms—the one in front had a little woodstove and a long table for sorting the mail. Maggie had been sitting at the table eating her lunch, pilot crackers and peanut butter.

She sat back down again and asked them if they were hungry. Buddy and Will were, so she pushed the box of pilot crackers across the table to them

and opened the can of peanut butter. She took a jackknife out of her pants pocket and wiped the blade on her shirt.

"Use this," she said, and Will took the knife to spread peanut butter on his cracker. Maggie inspected Graf while she chewed and swallowed. "Got some Indian in you. How old are you?"

Bo could see that Graf wasn't going to answer, so she said, "We don't know yet because his folks are dead. But Hank—he's a marshal—he's trying to find out when's his birthday."

"Whoa," said Buddy, impressed. "I never heard of anyone didn't know his own birthday."

"Shoot," said Maggie. "Old days, my mama told me, no one knew their birthday, just winter, spring, summer, fall. That's all they knew." She got up and put the crackers and peanut butter on a shelf and asked over her shoulder, "That new boy out the Willard dredge. You meet him yet?"

"No," said Will. "We just heard he was there. You see him?"

"No. Guys from Willard was telling me about him."

"There's two kids I haven't met," said Bo. "That

boy and Edna. I thought there would be more kids here, but that makes only six. I hope they come to town soon. There were fifteen kids at Ballard Creek."

"I suppose you want a girl to play with," Maggie said. She threw a look at Buddy and Will and laughed. "Well, our Edna isn't what you have in mind, I'll bet." Maggie ruffled Buddy's hair. "I had six brothers, and I never wanted no sisters. Boys are more fun, you know."

"Here comes Charlie," Buddy said, and Bo could hear the wagon crunching across the tailings. He didn't stop at the front door of the post office; he went around to the back where Maggie kept the mail. Maggie opened the freight door, and Charlie looked down at her from the seat on the wagon.

"Here's the freight came last night," Charlie said. "That box the boss at Kilbourne's been waiting for."

"Good, won't have to hear him carrying on anymore about how late it is," Maggie said. She strode to the back of the wagon, picked up the big box with a grunt, carried it into the back room, thumped it down on the floor, and dusted her hands. Buddy and Will gave Bo a see-what-we-told-you look.

Before Charlie went back to the horse barn, Bo

stood on tiptoe to pet Goldie, whispering her name to see her ears twitch. When she took her hand away, Goldie leaned her big head down and blew a prickly hot breath on Bo's cheek.

"That's how she says thank you," Charlie told her.

Then the boys took Bo and Graf to see a mama who lived alone with her grown daughter, down at the end of the tailing piles, the other end of town.

"She's blind, Nita's girl," said Will as they walked.

Bo had never seen anyone who was blind. Except Olaf's old dog at Ballard Creek. In the sun you could see that he had blue circles clouding his eyes.

"How'd she get that way?"

"Born like that," said Buddy, "but she can do lots of things."

"You should see her sew, and she can cook, too, just feels things with her hands. She comes walking with us lots, down to the creek and all."

When they got to the house, Will introduced them in what Bo thought was a very grown-up way.

"This is Nita Paniyak and her daughter named Paulie. And this is Bo and Graf. They used to live on the Koyukuk."

Bo was delighted to see that Nita was Eskimo. Someone to speak Eskimo with!

But as soon as Bo rattled off a few sentences, Nita looked startled and laughed.

"Oh, my," she said, and put her palms against her cheeks. "That's another kind of Eskimo," she said. "We live far away from those people, speak Yup'ik down where I come from."

Bo was very disappointed.

"I didn't know there were two kinds of Eskimo," said Bo. "Me and Graf speak Eskimo like the people in Ballard Creek, but we don't have anyone to talk to now. Just ourselves."

"Same with me," said Nita. "No one to talk to. I never talked Eskimo to Paulie, and now I'm sorry."

Bo and Nita traded some words, but there weren't any that were the same.

Paulie's eyes wandered around, and when she talked to them, she looked at the ceiling. She got up in a careful way, filled the teakettle, and set it on the stove. "We'll have some tea," she said.

She took six teacups from the shelf and set them on the table next to the sugar bowl, and then, using a finger to find the precise place, she carefully put a cup full of spoons next to the sugar bowl.

Paulie asked lots of questions about life in Ballard Creek. She touched Graf, to see how tall he was, and then she softly touched Bo's hair, felt her long braids.

"What color is your hair?"

Bo didn't know how you told about color to someone who couldn't see.

But Nita said, "Like the tall grass that grows down by the creek. Light, not dark like our hair."

"Oh," said Paulie. "Like straw."

"That's right," said Nita. "Swedish kind of hair, people call it."

"Are you Swedish?" asked Paulie.

"I don't know," said Bo. "I'm adopted. Me and Graf."

Nita looked at her gravely, and Paulie searched the ceiling with her dark darting eyes.

"I'm adopted too," said Nita. "But I always knew my real parents. They just had too many kids, so they gave me to someone who didn't have any."

"That's how it was in Ballard," Bo said. "Gracie already had one baby, so she gave her new baby to Dishoo and Big Jim."

"So who are your mother and father now?"

"We have two papas and no mamas," Bo said as she always did, hoping she wouldn't have to explain too much.

"Oh," said Nita calmly, not surprised. "Who braids your hair so beautifully?"

"Oh, both of my papas can braid hair. Except Jack always does it tighter." Bo put her fingers at the outside corners of her eyes and tugged. "He pulls my eyes tight, like this," she said.

BO AND GRAF left the boys at Nita's and made their way home across the tailings.

Bo was thinking about what it would be like to have an older brother like Will. Will talked more than Buddy and ordered him around. When Buddy agreed with Will, he said "yeah," but when he didn't, he argued hotly. Bo smiled. She liked it that Buddy could stick up for himself.

Arvid had been busy. He'd made four new long shelves that wrapped around the kitchen corner by

the back door. And by the couch he'd made a shelf
for their books and gramophone records.

Jack had just come back from the store, and he
set Bo and Graf to unwrapping a lot of packages tied
in red string. "Don't cut the string," Jack warned.
He was a devoted string saver.

Bo and Graf handed him the cans, and Jack
stacked them on the shelves in a certain strict order.
Alphabetical.

"Don't want to waste time looking for stuff," he said.

"What'd you and the boys do today?" Arvid asked.

"Buddy and Will didn't believe about Olaf's animals," Bo told him.

"*Is* hard to believe," Jack said. "Need to get a picture. Too bad no one in Ballard has a camera."

They were almost finished with the house. Arvid put up pegs on the bedroom walls to hang things on. When their clothes were all hung on the pegs, you couldn't see much wall.

Jack put curtains up in the kitchen and living room, the red and white ones he'd made for the cookshack in Ballard long ago. It made Bo feel happy to look at them.

The summer sun came in at the kitchen window and slid across the new table, and the shiny clean little house was already like home.

But they would never, not ever, get used to the sound of the dredge.

CHAPTER EIGHT

HOUSE WITH THE GREEN ROOF

BO AND GRAF were more curious about the people who lived in the house with the green roof than they were about anyone else. That house was quiet—no smoke from the chimney, not a sign of anyone since they'd moved in. Buddy and Will told them the men who lived there were out at the mining camp where Edna lived, doing some work for a few days.

But the next morning, Buddy and Will were grinning when they came to collect Bo and Graf. "They're back," Will said. "Come on!"

Bo and Graf hurried to finish the dishes while Buddy and Will ate the rest of the biscuits.

When they were going out the door, Will said, "They're both Finns, Stig and Eero. Only Finns we got here. We got lots of Irishmen and Montenegrins and a zillion other countries, but only two Finns."

"Oh," said Bo happily. "We have Finns in Ballard Creek. Arvid always says Finns are more stubborn than Swedes."

Will looked perplexed. "Is that a good thing?"

Bo stopped walking and looked at him uncertainly. "Well, I thought it was."

When Will tapped on the open screen door, Bo looked up at the green roof. It was tin just like their roof, but it had been painted that beautiful color. Bo didn't know you could paint tin roofs.

One old man was alone in the house, sitting at the table. He was Eero, short and round and bald.

"These here are the new kids. Bo and Graf. Got two papas and no mama," Will said, pleased to have something unusual to tell Eero.

"And one papa is a nigger, and one is a Swede," Buddy said just as proudly, for the same reason.

The smile fell off the old man's face as he swiveled his head to look at Buddy.

"That's a bad word," Eero said slowly. *"Nigger."*

Buddy and Will stared at Eero, dismayed. Bo looked uneasily from the boys to the old man and back again.

"I never knew it was bad," Buddy said.

Will looked at Eero pleadingly. "Everybody always called, you know, Nigger George that."

"Everybody," said Eero in a disgusted way. "Don't want to go through life doing what everybody does. If everybody does something, you can be pretty sure you don't want to be doing it."

Eero glared at the boys for a minute and then he ran his hand over his shiny head. "I know you didn't mean nothing," he said, his voice kinder. "Just let that be the last time you use that word. Ever."

Will and Buddy nodded, still looking uncomfortable.

Bo looked from face to face, not understanding anything. "What's a nigger?"

Will looked at Eero anxiously before he answered. "You know, like your papa. Dark."

"What do you call people who're not dark?"

Will looked at Eero again, but Eero just looked back at him, his eyebrows raised, waiting for him to answer. Will made a puzzled face and lifted his shoulders. "Just regular people, I guess."

Eero rolled his eyes, but Bo nodded. Another thing to ask the papas.

Eero'd been working with two pieces of rope, joining them together into a long piece. He gestured for them to take a seat around the table.

"This is called splicing," he told Bo and Graf. "Better learn how to do this. Never can tell when a rope'll give out on you." They watched him for a few minutes while he twisted the strands of rope together.

"Bo," he said thoughtfully. "In Finland that's a boy's name. Lots of Bos in Finland." Bo had nothing to say to that, because she wasn't sure whether she liked to have a boy's name.

"Eero taught me and Buddy to do knots," said Will. "I know sixteen different kinds now."

"Well, I know fourteen," Buddy said.

Eero stopped splicing.

"Maybe time for you to learn knots too?" he said to Graf. Graf looked startled and then pleased, so Eero picked up a short piece of rope and began to show Graf a knot.

"Cut some bread," he told the boys, not looking up from the knot. Buddy looked happy.

"Eero makes really good bread," he told Bo. The bread was dark and had little seeds in it that Bo didn't like. She put a lot of butter on her piece, and it tasted better.

"Jack makes bread different," she said.

"This is sour rye," Eero said. "Finnish rye. Takes some getting used to. Buddy here, he can't get enough, but Will don't like it."

The knot was called a bowline, and while they ate their bread, and Buddy cut himself some more,

Eero showed Graf each step over and over, slowly. When after a few tries, Graf got the knot to pull tight with the right-sized loop at the bottom, he gave them all a joyful look.

"Do that a couple times a day till your fingers know it without your thinking," said Eero. "No sense learning things with your brain. Got to learn them with your fingers. Unless your fingers got it memorized, your brain will forget it quick."

Eero didn't offer to teach Bo knots, and Bo was glad, because she was pretty sure she'd never be able to do it at all.

Another old man came in the door carrying a package wrapped in brown paper. Bo knew it came from the store because it was tied with red string like the packages the papas had brought home.

He was just the opposite of Eero, very tall and thin, almost as tall as Jack and Arvid. But kind of bent over like the tall reeds that grew along the creek at Ballard. He set the package on the dresser under the window and then held his hand out to Bo.

"Stig Koskinen," he said. Then he bent very low to shake Graf's hand. Stig jerked his head at Bo.

"Your mother?" he asked Graf.

Graf didn't get a joke very often, but this time he laughed at Stig. Then he said, "She's my sister. Bo."

Bo felt a funny pinch in her chest. *My sister.* It was the first time he'd ever said that.

Stig poured himself a cup of coffee from the pot on the woodstove and sat down next to Bo. His hair was a wild crop of white, and he had thick bushy eyebrows that went every which way.

"Bo—" he started, but Bo interrupted him.

"I know. Eero told me. It's a boy's name in Finn country." She looked at him from underneath her eyebrows.

Stig laughed. "I got a feeling you don't like that very much," he said. "But in lots of places, it's ordinary for names to be all mixed up. Lots of Eskimo names are for both boys and girls, you know. Used to always name a baby for someone just died, and so they had names could be used for both sexes. Baby was supposed to be that person come back to the world, see."

Bo looked startled. "Our Eskimos didn't do that," she said. "At least I don't think so."

"Your Eskimos?" Stig asked.

"Where we come from, Ballard Creek," she said.

"Oh, those are a different kind of Eskimo. Kobuk Eskimos, speak Inupiaq. I was talking about Yup'ik, down where me and Eero used to mine."

"That's what Paulie's mother said," Bo told him. "I never knew before that there were more kinds of Eskimos than our kind."

"You speak Eskimo?" asked Stig.

"Oh yes," said Bo. "And Graf, too."

"Good to grow up where there's more than one language," said Stig. "Your age, I could speak Finnish and Saami."

"What's Saami?"

"They live where I was raised," said Stig. "Some people call them Lapps. Tell you all about them sometime."

"Some Lapps came to Ballard Creek when I was sick last year," Bo said.

"Reindeer herders," said Stig. "Lapps is a name other people gave them. They don't like it. They're Saami. People got a right to be called what they want to be called."

Bo nodded. She thought so too.

She was learning a lot visiting the people in Iditarod Creek.

There were newspapers glued carefully over all the walls. A lot of the old cabins in Ballard Creek had been papered in newspapers to keep the warm in, but Bo could tell the ones on Stig and Eero's walls weren't in English. "Are those Finn newspapers?" she asked.

"Right," said Stig. "Finnish, you say."

"Nels Niemi back home was a Finn, a Finnish man," said Bo. "His sister Asa came to live with him last year, and everyone said he was lucky to have a partner who could cook."

Eero and Graf had their heads together, almost touching. Eero was showing Graf another knot—the half-hitch—and he didn't look up when he said, "Good to have a partner."

Stig poured himself more coffee. "Your papas been partners for long? Me and Eero been partners for thirty-five years."

"Oh my," said Bo. It sounded like a forever long time to her. She twisted one of her braids to help her think. "My papas weren't partners before they got me. Jack said he and Arvid just partnered up the minute they got me because they knew I wasn't going to be a one-man job."

"Well, that's how partners is," Stig said. "Don't partner up till you've got a job too big for one. Sometimes one of you works for a grubstake while the other is out prospecting. Hard country without a partner. Need someone to watch your back."

"The man Ballard Creek is named after—he got eaten by a bear, and so all the men in the mine named Ballard Creek for him. His partner still lives there, and he still misses him," Bo said.

Stig took a sip of his coffee. "Course, partners don't always get along. Split up more often than not."

"My papas are good-natured," Bo told him, thinking of what Will had said.

"Good-natured is about the best you can get in a partner," said Stig. "Beats strong, or smart, or honest, or rich."

Eero raised his eyebrow at Stig.

"Well," said Stig, "maybe good-natured don't beat rich."

"My best friend at Ballard Creek was Oscar," Bo told them. "Everyone used to say *we* were partners. I wish I could write him a letter, but I don't know how to write yet. My papas said they'd write it for me when they get time."

"Well, now," said Stig. "Here's a man with plenty of time. That's me. Living right next door to you. You just come here and tell me what you want to say, and I'll write it down. You can take it to the post office, and it'll be off to Ballard Creek in the next mail plane."

Bo felt a rush of happiness.

"Yes," said Bo. "Oh yes, thank you."

THAT NIGHT when Bo and Graf and the papas were finishing dinner, she remembered some of the questions she'd been meaning to ask the papas. "What's Athabascan?"

"That's a kind of Indian here in Alaska. Like those people at the wood camps and the fish camps," Jack said. "Likely Graf here is part Athabascan."

Jack had a cigar Hardy had given him, and he was doing something interesting to the end of it with his pocket knife. "There's Eskimos and Indians, you know. Different ways. Different talk," Jack said.

"And what's a Canuck, then?"

"That's a name for someone from Canada." He looked up at her. "Why you asking?"

"That's what Will and Buddy said Maggie and Frenchie were," Bo said. "Athabascan and Canuck. There are a lot of names for what kind of person you are, aren't there? Like when Sandor used to call Tomas a Polack. That meant where he came from, I forget the name of the country. And Buddy said you were a nigger. But it didn't mean where you were from. He said it was the word for brown people like you."

In the sudden stillness when Jack and Arvid looked at each other, Graf scowled at his fork and growled, "Eero said *nigger* is a bad word."

Arvid looked grim.

"Mmmm, mmm, *mmmmm*," hummed Jack, which meant there was something to deal with.

He held a match to his cigar and puffed on it till the end glowed.

After he blew out the smoke, Jack said, "Sometimes *nigger* surely is a mean word. Sometimes it's just a word. Like when Will said it."

Jack gave them his two-dimple smile, his that's-just-the-way-it-is smile. "You know, there's a lot of mean words out there. A lot. No end to mean names."

Bo and Graf were frowning at the papas, troubled.

"Guess you two didn't know there were mean people in the world," Arvid said sadly.

Bo and Graf looked at each other. "Miz Eller," Graf said, pointing his chin in the direction of the Eller house.

Jack and Arvid grinned delightedly. They'd already heard a lot about Miz Eller.

"Right!" said Arvid. "Miz Eller. Now, she's the kind wouldn't use mean names 'cause it's not genteel, but she's mean every other kind of way. There's genteel meanness and plain meanness."

"I swear I'd rather deal with plain meanness," Jack said with a laugh. "Any day of the year."

CHAPTER NINE

THE DREDGE

ARVID AND JACK went to work on the dredge as soon as they were settled in the house. They'd lost so many weeks of work traveling to Iditarod Creek they had no time to waste. Jack worked nights. He got home from the dredge at six in the morning just as Arvid was ready to walk out the door to do his day shift.

First thing when he got home, Jack had to repair the damage. Arvid always left the kitchen in an uproar when he cooked breakfast for himself—scrambled eggs burnt on the bottom of the skillet, pools of ketchup on the table, oatmeal spilled on the floor, and the bread sliced all crooked. Jack truly hated it when anyone sliced the bread crooked.

While Bo and Graf were eating breakfast, Jack's bread dough would rise, and as soon as breakfast was over and the dishes were done, Jack would put the loaves in the oven to bake while Bo and Graf did the dusting.

There was always dust over everything because the wind blew dirt off the tailing piles, and there was no green thing growing to hold it down.

Jack hated ordinary dust bad enough, but this dust was something special. "God almighty," Jack grumbled. "Never saw the like. Dust, and two minutes later, it's all over everything again. And gritty to boot."

Jack bought two feather dusters at Sidney Cohen's store. Bo and Graf had never seen a feather duster before, and they thought of a lot of things to do with them—like playing war—when Jack wasn't looking. Which sort of got the dust all scattered around again.

They skittery-skattered the dusters along the windowsills where the dust lay the thickest and along the shelves in the living room. They dusted the chair rungs and the top of the wood box and everyplace else that dust could come to rest.

But even standing on a chair, Bo couldn't dust the new shelves Arvid had made in the kitchen. So Jack did that, which Bo thought was fair, because he and Arvid were the only ones who could see the dust up there.

Jack had to go to sleep at noon so he could get up and go to work again at six. Bo and Graf could go out in the afternoon, and they had plenty to do in the house as well—quiet things that wouldn't wake Jack up. So it worked out fine.

Jack left for his shift as soon as Arvid came home to eat dinner with Bo and Graf, the dinner that Jack had been cooking on the back of the stove all day.

Bo had a lot to tell Arvid every night while they were having supper.

Arvid always said he didn't know how she ever got a mouthful, she was so busy talking. Graf mostly just shook his head to agree or said "yeah" once in a while. But every so often, he'd put his fork down and stare at Bo.

"Uh-*uh*," he'd say, meaning that's not right. And he'd tell his side of the story.

Arvid sawed wood every night and then he split it and made kindling while Graf filled the wood box. Bo washed the supper dishes while she played records, and after the chores, there was time to play checkers or take a walk.

Then Arvid got them washed up and in bed, shiny clean and tired, and read them something from a magazine till they fell asleep.

ONE MORNING Jack took Bo and Graf to watch the dredge work.

The dredge made such a shocking noise up close that both Bo and Graf put their hands over their ears.

The dredge was longer than anything Bo and Graf had seen before. Longer than the scow on the Koyukuk, longer than the sternwheelers they'd seen on the Yukon.

The huge house thing on it was covered with tin, and the sun glared off of it so brightly they could hardly look at it.

The dredge sat on a barge that floated on metal balloons—pontoons—on the dredge pond. There was a long metal rod called a spud on the front of the dredge, which twisted itself into the ground, loosening the gravel. Then the barge swung screeking to the left side, and another spud came out to grind some more.

When there was a lot of loose gravel, a line of dredge buckets slammed and rattled down a moving ladder, and each bucket tipped forward to scoop up the dirt the spud had loosened. Then the bucket slid underneath the ladder and another bucket took its place in front.

Bo tried to count how many buckets were lined up, scooping, pulling the buckets to the inside of the dredge. She had to give up because they never sat still. Jack told her there were thirty-six.

At the same time that the buckets were pulling gravel inside the dredge, gravel was spitting out the back, making more tailing piles.

Jack had to bend way down and shout in her ear. "That gravel going out the back," said Jack, "that's what's been sluiced already, has the gold washed out of it."

Graf was looking miserable with all the noise and clanking. It *was* upsetting, Bo thought.

Jack shouted some more. "The sluice boxes are inside there. The gold drops down to the bottom of the sluice boxes, just like at Ballard Creek. Except what took us months to do there takes an hour here."

In Ballard Creek, the men went underground down a long shaft with their picks and shovels to dig. Then they'd put that pay dirt in a bucket to haul up to the top of the shaft with steam power. That was called drift mining.

"That dirt we moved in Ballard? What took us one winter, they do in a week here with the dredge. In one summer, it can chew up and spit out that whole valley there, all the gravel the town is on now."

He laughed at the look on Bo's face. "I can't believe it myself," he said. "And I don't much like the whole idea. Look at the mess it makes."

"Doesn't it ever stop?" asked Bo.

"Just a few minutes every day. We can go look at what's inside later. Maybe Arvid will be working in there today. First we'll go up to the cookshack and you can meet Louise. She's the cook. And the boys. They'll just be eating now."

In the cookshack, Jack introduced Bo and Graf to all the men who sat eating at long tables. Not as many as the men at Ballard Creek.

"I thought there would be more of them," Bo said.

"Don't forget they run two shifts here," said Jack. "And remember, it don't take so many men to mine as it did at Ballard."

All the men had something to say and looked so happy to see them that Bo felt at home right away.

"Sit right down by me," one man said, scooting over on his bench. "How about some cake or pie? Louise makes a rollicking good pie."

When the cook set two pieces of pumpkin pie down in front of them, Jack said, "This here is Louise. Don't give her no trouble, or she'll thump you!" Bo could tell Jack was kidding because of the way Louise was smiling.

She was a plump woman, covered in a huge apron. She bent and touched Bo's cheek with one finger.

"I have a granddaughter just your age," she said. Then she went back to the counter to get another piece of pie for Jack.

The men were almost as noisy as the bunch at Ballard Creek, Bo thought happily. They kept asking questions: How did they like the trip on the river? Were they in cahoots with Buddy and Will, getting up to no good? Did your brother knock out that tooth? Was Jack ever mean? Just tell them, and they would fix things.

Bo was delighted with them, but Graf was not happy. He began to growl in Eskimo, talking to the table like he always did. "Too noisy," he was complaining. Bo told him it was just the same back home. Didn't he remember when everyone was in the cookshack?

"What's that you're talking?" asked the man who was sitting next to them.

"Eskimo," said Bo. Some of the men began to laugh.

"Well, now, I never took Jack here for no Eskimo!"

Jack's laugh crashed out, and all the men laughed with him. Bo could see that they all loved teasing as much as the boys at Ballard Creek had.

After the men had clumped out of the cookshack to go back to work, Jack introduced them to Archie. Archie—a little man with wispy gray hair—was the dishwasher, like their Gitnoo had been back home.

Bo and Graf were startled when Archie walked toward them, bobbing and limping.

"Archie froze his feet in overflow when he was

driving dogs to the coast," Jack said. The little man nodded at them in agreement. "They cut off all his toes at the hospital."

Bo's stomach lurched.

"See, I can walk without toes," Archie said, "but I'm very tippy. I stuff the toes of my boots with extra socks, and that helps, but I still got to be careful. Can't go racing or nothing. I'll show you," he said, and he sat down on a low stool and started to unlace his boots.

"No," said Bo in a horrified way. "It always makes my stomach go all funny when I see some-one's hurts."

Archie looked disappointed, but he stopped unlacing.

"Going to show them inside the dredge now," said Jack.

"Come back, come back anytime and visit," Archie said.

Bo smiled at him. He really was very nice. "Thank you," she said. She elbowed Graf.

"Thank you," said Graf. Then he said, "*I* wanted to see your feet."

INSIDE THE DREDGE, it was too noisy to bear. It made Bo feel a little sick.

They met the dredgemaster and the dredge crew, all of them bustling about. Arvid, they said, was out at the shop.

One of the oilers looked as if he'd taken a bath in oil.

"That's my job when I'm on shift," Jack said.

"You never look that dirty," said Bo.

"I take a shower and change my clothes before I come home," said Jack. "Can't stand being that dirty one minute longer than it takes."

It was just too noisy in the dredge for them to take much in.

"It feels as if the noise is making my brain stop," Bo yelled into Jack's ear.

"Well, now you've seen one of the wonders of the world," Jack yelled back. "Let's go home."

A FEW DAYS LATER, Jack told them at breakfast there was a surprise for them at the mining camp. The men who'd been in the kitchen when they visited the dredge had made swings for them. He'd take them after their chores were finished to see it.

"Oh!" said Bo. She looked at Graf, wide-eyed. They'd only seen those men once. "That was very nice of them, wasn't it, Papa?"

"Funny place here, Iditarod Creek, with hardly any kids. Everyone gets homesick for kids," said Jack.

The swing frame was made of peeled spruce poles, still slick with sap, and had two beautifully sanded seats, smooth as velvet. It stood on the edge of a tailing pile, and you could swing way far out over the edge and look so far down that Bo felt a little dizzy.

They were wonderful swings, and Jack showed Bo how to pump so she could go higher. They still had to push Graf, of course.

There wasn't much time in the morning for swinging, but often after dinner, Arvid took them to the dredge. The men who'd built the swing would come out of the bunkhouse and hunker down with their pipes and cigarettes and watch them play.

Almost all of them took a turn on it, too. Bo thought that maybe swinging was something you didn't get too old to do.

CHAPTER TEN

IDITAROD CREEK LADIES

BUDDY AND WILL hadn't been able to play for a while because their ma was doing spring cleaning, and she had a hundred things for the boys to do. Spring cleaning, Buddy said, was when you took every single thing in the house and put it in the middle of the floor and washed it and then you put it back.

"And then when everything is washed, Ma don't hardly want us around. Every time we come in the house, she yells, 'Clean your feet!'" The boys hated spring cleaning.

But finally their ma was finished, and the boys came bounding up to the door again. "Come on!" Will said, and they all followed him, running across the tailings.

The boys were showing them what used to be the dance hall, all boarded up now, when a woman came around the corner of the building and called out to them. Will stopped so short that Buddy ran into him.

"*Uh*-oh," said Will under his breath.

The woman made a come-here gesture. "Introduce me to your new friends," she sang out brightly.

Will and Buddy slid a horrified look at each other, but they stopped and took their hats off.

She was Miz Forney, Will said. She wore a flow-ered dress, and her elbows, Bo noticed, were very pointy. She was pleasant and spoke very sweetly, but as she asked them questions, Bo could tell she knew the answers already.

Will and Buddy had gone stony faced, stiff backed, and as soon as Miz Forney had finished her questions, they tugged their caps on again and got Bo and Graf out of there.

After they were out of sight of Miz Forney, Buddy

and Will made faces at each other. Bo and Graf watched them, bewildered.

"Why did you take your hats off?" Graf asked.

Will stopped and put his hands on his hips. "See, there's Miz Forney and Miz Littleton and Miz Shelton and Miz Roberts and our ma. That's what they call each other, too—Miz—because they think it's bad manners to call people by their first names. It's got to be Miz and Mister. And they say a man is supposed to take his hat off when he talks to a woman. Which is the most foolish thing I ever heard of. And Ma makes us do it."

Buddy nodded energetically. "Yeah," he complained.

Will was wound up now. "And they have a tea party every week, get dressed up. I hate it when it's at our house. Ma cleans like a crazy woman and kicks us out and won't let us eat any of the cake she makes, and when it's over, she's all hoity-toity with Pa and tells him he should change his dirty work shirt when he comes home so we'll grow up civilized and not think it's okay to be all covered with tailing dust and oil."

"Yeah," Buddy grumbled.

"They don't like kids much, the Mizzes," Will said, starting to walk on. "Ma's the only one with kids, and she says we're an embarrassment to her."

Bo and Graf were beginning to think that Will and Buddy had things pretty hard.

They had come to the boardwalk, a long path made of wooden planks, which snaked between the tailing piles and ran down along the creek. The rough boards smelled good in the sun, the way the log cabins in Ballard smelled on a hot day.

The boys pointed out Emma and Tom's house, the first house along the boardwalk.

"Tom's the dredgemaster over at the Kilbourne dredge. He's a really good guy," Buddy said.

"He's got a prodigious big scar on the side of his face," Will said, bragging, and he drew a long, crooked line with his forefinger from his hairline to his chin. Bo was very interested in that. She'd never seen anyone with a big scar.

A soft-looking woman with a fat twist of pale biscuit-colored hair was hanging her wet laundry on a clothesline by the house. She waved at the boys and came to the fence.

"Here's the new kids," Will said. Emma shook

their hands. "Me and Tom were sure happy to hear we had some more kids in town," she said fervently. "You come and see me anytime."

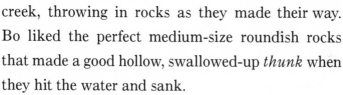

After they left, Buddy said, "Ma don't like Emma because she used to be a good-time girl. But *we* like her."

They left the boardwalk and walked along on the edge of the creek, throwing in rocks as they made their way. Bo liked the perfect medium-size roundish rocks that made a good hollow, swallowed-up *thunk* when they hit the water and sank.

Graf liked to watch the rings spread out in a circle, so any rock would do, but the other boys were only interested in finding the perfect flat rock for skipping. Buddy said the trouble with *that* was when you found a perfect rock, you had to throw it away.

Will was the best at skipping. He made them all stop throwing rocks in the water while he did it. "Gotta have the water perfectly smooth," he said. Once he made six skips, but he couldn't do it again.

Bo suddenly pointed. "What's that?"

There was an oily slick in the water, a shimmering rainbow.

"Diesel. From the dredge pond," said Will. "Leaks over into the creek sometimes."

"What's diesel?"

The boys looked at her pityingly. "That's what they run the dredge with," Buddy said, looking as if he couldn't believe she'd asked that question.

"Oh," said Bo, feeling stupid. "In Ballard they used steam to run the boiler and the winch and things."

"That's really old-fashioned," Will said in a superior way. Bo felt hurt for Ballard Creek.

"Well, at least steam doesn't get into the water," she said. She still felt stung. "Or make such a clang-clang-god-rotted-clankety-clank noise!" she said, thinking about what Arvid had called that sound. Both Will and Buddy stopped and looked at her, delighted. "Clang-clang-god-rotted-clankety-clank!" they said to each other over and over.

After they left the creek bank, Will announced cheerfully, "Edna's leaving on the mail plane with her ma tomorrow. Going back where they live Outside. Going early this year."

Bo stopped in her tracks and gave him a cross look. "I never even got to see her close up," said Bo.

"Well, if you had, she would have bossed you around right away," said Will. "She's the bossiest person I ever saw, even more than Ma."

"Yeah," said Buddy.

"But you remember that kid at Willard dredge we told you about? Dave—he's a friend of our pa, works at the Willard mine—he was telling us about him last night."

"How old is he?" asked Graf. Graf was very interested in ages because he didn't know his.

"Dave said some older than me, maybe not much. Said they never see him because his pop makes sure he don't hang around the boys much."

"What's his name?" Bo asked.

"Dave don't even know. He never talked to the kid, and Dave said his pa's strange. A grouch."

"I wish he could play with us," said Bo wistfully. She'd never get used to having so few children around.

"Not likely," Will said. "Willard mine is too far away—that's why you don't see the miners from Willard very often. Got to be pretty important to walk the ten miles, five here and five back."

They were getting sweaty and dusty in the afternoon sun, so Will said it was a good time to go to the hotel. And, he said, there was always something there to eat.

It was cool and dark inside the hotel. For a minute, Bo could hardly see after the bright sunshine, but when she could, she saw Nita sitting at a card table back by the bar with three ladies and an old man. They were all being very noisy, carrying on and insulting one another.

Will laughed. "They're playing five-card-stud poker. That's Nita's favorite game." Will led them to a table nearby and introduced them to the old miner named Trolly and to the good-time girls, Carmen and Sadie and Little Jill.

The girls teased Buddy and Will and made a big fuss over Bo and Graf, insisting that they all sit down and have a glass of Hardy's strawberry Kool-Aid. Bo thought strawberry Kool-Aid was the most beautiful drink she'd ever imagined, but Graf took

one sip and pushed his glass away. Bo looked a question at him, and he said, "Too red." Whatever that meant.

Little Jill had beautiful dark orange curls. "Your hair is the same color as one of my crayons," Bo told her. "Burnt sienna."

Sadie was very different. She had jet-black hair cut very short in the back like the women in catalogs, straight shiny bangs across her forehead. They both looked fancier than Carmen, who had her hair tied back with a scarf.

Bo thought Carmen was the nicest of all.

It was the way her eyes looked when she listened, as if she was feeling things all the way down into her stomach. And the way she brushed Graf's hair back out of his eyes and the way she buttoned Bo's overall strap that was hanging loose. The boys had told her Carmen was the person everyone sent for if they got sick or if there was a broken bone to set. Bo could see that she was the kind of person who wanted to take care of you.

"Tell us how you came to get your papas," Little Jill said. So Bo told them the story—as much as she had patience for, because it seemed she'd been telling it a lot lately.

Carmen tipped her head at the other girls. "We didn't have much luck in the father department," she said. "You're very lucky kids."

CHAPTER ELEVEN

VISITORS

A LOT OF THE BOYS from the nearby mines came to visit the papas when they were in town for one reason or another. Some had known Jack or Arvid at different diggings over the years, and there was a lot of talk remembering this and remembering that. What Bo liked best were the stories of the old gold rush days. Stig had a lot of them.

Once when Jack was kneading the day's batch of bread, Stig said, "Puts me in mind of the time all our flour got wet when we were rafting down the Stikine. All winter we had to take an ax to that flour and chop off a chunk and then we had to slam that chunk with the sledgehammer to powder it enough just to make some bannocks. I think about that every time I dip into the flour barrel to make bread."

"Why didn't you just buy some more flour?" Bo asked.

Stig laughed. "We was way out in the bush, nowhere to buy nothing, and even if we hadn't been, we didn't have no money, and even if we had money, we couldn't buy flour because there was none left anywhere in the country. Too many stampeders came, everyone about starving. So we figured we was lucky, even if we had to pound on it to bake anything."

Everyone laughed, but Bo was thinking that if there was ever another gold rush, *she* wasn't going to go.

Will and Buddy's dad, Ben, visited sometimes. Bo liked him because he laughed so much. And Emma's husband, Tom, came one morning. He greeted the other men cheerfully and put his hand out to Bo and Graf. "My Em was very pleased to meet you," he said.

Bo and Graf had gone motionless, frozen, because there in front of them was the scar they'd heard about. It was purple and enormous, stretched all ropy from the top of his scalp, down the side of his face, under his nose, making his top lip a little wobbly, and down the other cheek where it ended just under his jaw.

Tom smiled at them in an understanding way. "I always have to wait for someone to get their fill of this first," he said, "before they'll say anything to me. I used to be the most ordinary guy you ever saw, before I got this. Now I'm famous. Bet Em never would have married me if I'd had my ordinary face."

Bo remembered her manners and held her hand out to Tom. "It's very nice," said Bo, politely.

"Did it hurt?" rasped Graf.

Tom looked at Graf, surprised.

"It did," he said vehemently. "Hurt like a—" He stopped suddenly and darted an alarmed look at the boys around the table. "Like a really bad thing," he finished lamely.

They'd met four of the Charlies now. Charlie the Tram was their first Charlie, and three more had come to their house: Good-Time Charlie, who liked to dance; Charlie Hootch, who made whiskey; and Dago Charlie, which meant he was Italian, Jack said.

Five more Charlies to go.

ONE DAY FRENCHIE asked Bo, "Ever see this kid out at the Willard mine?"

"No," she said. "Buddy and Will heard he was there, but they've never seen him either. Did you?"

"Yeah, when I was hauling some pipe out to the Willard diggings. Kid just gave me a sideways smile and melted away, not looking for conversation, I guess. Guys at Willard's say they hardly see him. Say his dad hired the kid out to the cook to split the wood, and he sleeps in the shed at the cookshack. It don't seem right.

"The cook says the kid's polite, but don't say much. Cook asks him why he's so quiet, and the kid says, 'My pa don't like me talking to people.' The guys say his pa sure don't talk to anyone."

Bo and Graf looked puzzled at each other. Someone who didn't talk was not in their experience.

BO AND GRAF were finishing the supper dishes when they heard footsteps skittering in the gravel near their house. Buddy and Will for sure, though they usually didn't come after supper.

When Bo opened the door, she knew right away that the little curly-haired girl with them was Edna.

"Oh!" Bo said. "I'm so glad to see you! I'm Bo, and this is Graf. We saw you on the day we came. You were riding in the house."

Edna tossed her head. "That was fun," she said. "My ma had a fit."

She stared at Bo. "*I* have natural curly hair," she said. "*Your* hair is straight."

Then she inspected Graf. "Your brother doesn't look like you." Bo and Graf gave each other an uneasy look. No one had ever told them that before. Was that good or was it bad?

She pushed past Bo into the house and looked around.

"This is a very small house. I remember when the Andersons lived here."

She wandered around the living room.

"Our gramophone is much bigger than this one."

Arvid came out of the kitchen to say hello. Edna shook his hand briskly, then went behind him to examine that room.

"Your kitchen is small too. Ours is much bigger. And we have prettier dishes than that."

She looked at the cookie jar. "What kind of cookies are those?"

"Gingersnaps," said Arvid. "Jack's speciality."

"I don't like those," said Edna. "Don't you have another kind?"

Arvid gave her a sharp look and shook his head.

Edna strutted around the house, picking up this and that, but nothing found favor with her.

Buddy raised an eyebrow to show Bo what he thought of Edna's behavior.

Will looked grim, too. "Want to come out?" he asked. Graf and Bo looked uncomfortable and didn't answer, but Arvid saved them.

"Too late," he said. "Kids are just getting ready for bed."

"I told Edna that," said Will. "But she wanted to come anyway."

Edna tossed her head again. "Well, I'm leaving tomorrow. We're going back to our real home in

Washington tomorrow. It's a really big house, and we have an automobile—it's a Packard 740, Dual Cowl Phaeton—and I'm going to get a lot of new dresses." She looked at Bo. "Do you have any dresses?"

Bo gave Arvid a warning look and said no, though she really did have two of them hanging on the pegs in their bedroom. She had a feeling that this girl was not going to like her dresses.

When Edna had gone out the door, Will turned and made a face at Bo. "I *told* you she was bossy," he whispered.

When they were all gone, Arvid stood with his hands on his hips and a who'd-believe-it smile on his face. "Whoo-ee," was all he said.

CHAPTER TWELVE

TWO KINDS
OF WRITING

THERE WASN'T TIME to do all their laundry, even if they'd had a washing machine, which they didn't. So Arvid and Jack sent their washing to the laundry, like everyone else in town.

They would stuff everything into burlap bags, and Bo and Graf would pile those bags into the wagon and pull it to the Japanese laundry next to the hotel. Billows of steam hissed out of the back windows of the laundry from time to time, and then the whole street smelled of steam.

The Japanese men were amazed that most of the things in the burlap bags were not clothes.

"How much your papas change sheets and towels?" they asked. Bo and Graf had no idea. The Japanese men were surprised to find miners so clean and fussy about sheets and towels.

"It's just Jack," explained Bo. "Arvid doesn't pay any attention to stuff like that."

They were very clean themselves, the Japanese men, as particular as Jack. They took a bath in the steaming water of the laundry every day.

Their names were Haruto Hiroshi and Yoshihiro Ishikawa.

"I can't remember your names," said Bo despairingly one day. "They won't stick in my head!"

"Oh, that all right," said Haruto. "You call me Harry, you call him Yosh. That more easy."

Bo considered that. "I want to call you your real names," she said. "They're so pretty. But I keep losing hold of them. I get the first sound, and the rest just slides away."

"Here, I write them down for you. You practice," Yoshihiro said. Bo didn't tell him she didn't know how to read.

Yoshihiro wrote and then showed her. "These our name in English, and these our name in Japanese. Can't really write Japanese good with a pencil, but that's about right."

"You can write two kinds of ways," Bo said sadly. She was beginning to feel that she was behind in learning things.

Haruto got a little book off the shelf that he said was Japanese poetry, the words made the right way. Not with a pencil but with a brush.

Japanese writing was nothing like American writing. It was curvier and had thick places and thin ones, and each figure was like a picture or a design.

"Our kind of writing is not pretty," said Bo. "Not like yours." Yoshihiro and Haruto made a little bow with their heads and looked pleased.

"Take us long time to learn when we are little," Yoshihiro said. "Yours, just some straight lines and some round ones. Faster to learn."

Bo kept the piece of paper Yoshihiro had given her, and she and Graf tried to draw the Japanese names. It was very hard.

She practiced saying the names every night with Arvid. Graf didn't have to practice, because it turned out he'd learned them the first time he heard them.

But at last she had them just right.

"Can learn anything, you just set your mind to it," said Arvid. But Bo noticed he still hadn't learned them.

In the morning, when she showed Jack that she'd memorized Yoshihiro and Haruto's names, she asked, "Where is Japan, anyway?"

"Not so far," Jack said, and he showed her on the map that was pinned under the kitchen shelves. "Look, we're practically neighbors."

"I wonder if Yoshihiro and Haruto get homesick like we do for Ballard."

"Must be even worse," said Jack. "You moved away from Ballard, but you moved to a country almost the same. Same trees and birds, and everyone talks your language. Think how it would be to move to a place with all different trees and birds and animals, and everyone wears different clothes and talks different. And writes different. Be strange if they didn't get homesick."

Bo could see that some people had more to miss than she did.

CHAPTER THIRTEEN

THE STRAIGHT LADY

SOMETIMES JACK SENT BO and Graf to the store for matches or a can of milk or Ivory soap flakes for the dishes—whatever he'd run out of.

That was one of their favorite things to do, because the store man, Sidney Cohen, liked children very much and because he always had a treat for them. And besides, the store was full of wonderful things: a dozen kinds of knives and leather gloves that smelled interesting, snuff and snares and cigars.

Milo had a store in the roadhouse at Ballard, but he only got a new order twice a year on the scow. So everything in his store got tired and dusty, and there was never anything different. But at Sidney's, new things came on the plane every week in the summer.

One day when they went into the store, Sidney, wrapped in his big apron, his curly hair in a gray cloud around his head, was on the ladder getting something from the shelf.

He turned to give them his cheery greeting— "*Kinderle!*"—and when he climbed down, he said, "Have I got news for you! There's a new boy come into the country with his father. That makes five of you, or is it six?" He rolled his eyes up dramatically. "Before long, there will be children everywhere we look. No room on the sidewalks for grown-ups!"

Sidney always exaggerated.

"Will and Buddy told us," said Bo.

"Did they see him?" asked Sidney. Bo and Graf shook their heads. "I never saw him either," said Sidney. "Just the father. Italian, judging by his name."

Sidney was back on the ladder sort of talking to himself. "Not a pleasant person, the father. He's *meshugene*, I think. Crazy."

"That's four boys," said Bo. "But now Edna's gone, there's just me for girls."

"Do you wish you had a girl to play with, Bo?" Sidney asked kindly.

"Maggie asked me that," said Bo. "She said boys are more fun, and I think so too."

They stood at the counter on their tiptoes watching Sidney wrap the slab of bacon Jack had asked for, admiring the red string they liked so much, when a tall lady in a striped dress came in.

Bo and Graf looked her over carefully. Her hair was pulled back into a round sort of ball, and she had funny eyeglasses that pinched her nose and didn't go around her ears like the ones Tomas in Ballard Creek had. One of the tea party ladies Buddy and Will had told them about for sure.

She carried a big leather sort of bag with the handles over her arm. It was so big Bo thought it could hold a fat baby. She wished she could see what the woman had inside it.

While Sidney filled a little sack with salt from the big salt barrel, the lady stood very straight at the counter, her chin high. Her behind was straight, and

her front was straight as well, Bo noticed with interest. Bo had never seen a woman who wasn't puffy in front.

The straight lady waited silently. When Sidney turned to the counter, he nodded at her politely—"Miz Eller"—and continued to tie up the package of salt for Bo.

Bo and Graf shot each other a startled look. The binoculars lady!

"I need a pound of raisins and—" the lady started.

"When I'm finished with these customers," Sidney interrupted calmly.

Miz Eller looked down at Bo and Graf as if she'd not seen them there, her eyes cold.

"These must be the wards of that very odd partnership that's come to town."

"That's true," said Sidney, "though I'd probably call them children, and a better behaved pair of children I never did see."

"Early days, Mr. Cohen," Miz Eller said.

Bo didn't know what that meant. And what were wards?

"I am rather in a hurry, Mr. Cohen," Miz Eller said.

He smiled at her sweetly as if he hadn't heard what she said.

"And what else did your papa need, Bo?"

"Some maple flavoring," she said.

"Making syrup, is he?"

"He's making some maple bars for the dredge. Because the boys made us a swing."

"A swing! Now, that's a fine thing," Sidney said enthusiastically.

Bo could feel Miz Eller stiffen up next to her, and it was making her nervous. Bo turned to Graf and said in Eskimo, "I think I'm forgetting something."

"*Qaqqulaaq*," said Graf. Crackers.

Miz Eller's eyes narrowed into slits. "I heard about this. These children speak heathen languages."

Bo looked up at her. "No, it's Eskimo," she said. "Graf and I speak Eskimo."

Miz Eller's face stretched itself tight. "Do not speak until you're spoken to. Have you never been taught any manners?"

Bo couldn't think of anything to say to that, but when Sidney handed Bo the bacon and the other things, he said to Miz Eller, "I know no one with better manners than Bo."

Miz Eller gave him a cold look.

He smiled down at Bo. "And as a matter of interest, it might be said that I speak a heathen language as well," he told her. Before Bo could ask him what language that was, Sidney asked, "Can I get you anything else?"

"No," Bo said, even though Graf was reminding her again in Eskimo about the crackers. No one had ever looked at her in a mean way in her life, and she wanted to get away from Miz Eller's squinched-up eyes.

"Here then," said Sidney and he put a scoop of gumdrops from the glass jar on his countertop into a twist of paper. "Tell Jack to save me a maple bar," he said and smiled them out of the store.

Only when they'd reached the doorway did he turn to the woman, his palms flat on the counter. "Now then, Miz Eller?"

CHAPTER FOURTEEN

DOC LARUE

WILL AND BUDDY came banging on the door one morning. They had different kinds of knocks, but this kind was what Jack called their gangster knock, so they all knew it was something exciting.

"Doc Larue's in town!" they burst out at the same time when Jack opened the door. "You got to see him! He's real crazy!"

Bo looked a question at Jack.

Jack looked delighted. "Well, I'll be damned!" he

chortled. "That's the dentist, famous for crazy. He was at Ballard one time while you was just a baby."

"You never know what he's going to get up to," said Buddy.

"Me and Arvid run into him many times before," said Jack. "The Rampart camp and at Circle City before that. Turns up everywhere. Flies his own plane now." Jack smiled fondly. "Always had a bottle in his overalls pocket. Took a slug of whiskey from time to time while he was working on your teeth."

Jack got quiet all of a sudden and looked thoughtful. He took Bo's jaw in his big hand. "Open up."

Bo had lost her first tooth on the Yukon, coming from Ballard Creek, and just a week ago she'd lost another.

"Last tooth you lost, it's already got tiny little nubs of teeth poking up. Jaggedy little white edges here." Graf stood on tiptoe to see into Bo's mouth, and Buddy and Will gathered around to look too. Bo rolled her eyes from one to the other, mouth wide open.

"See," he said to Graf, "the teeth have little saws on the top to cut their way through the gum. Looks like this one is pushing hard to grow." Then Jack frowned at the space where Bo had lost the first tooth on the Yukon. "Nothing coming up here yet. Just a naked hole. Seems to be taking an unnatural long time, that new tooth. Think I'll take you to see what Doc has to say about it."

When he let her jaw go, Bo stood up on a chair to look in the little mirror over the washbasin. There was an empty space right in the front of her top teeth, a perfectly square empty space. Bo liked to stick her tongue through so it looked like she had one pink tooth.

THERE WERE A LOT of men at the hotel, waiting for Doc Larue. Some of them were playing cards with the old-timers; some were perched up on the bar stools, talking to one another.

Dago Charlie was there, and some of the boys from the Eller dredge, and a lot of loud and cheerful men Bo and Graf had never seen.

"And what's wrong with your teeth?" Dago Charlie asked her. "You're too young to have tooth troubles."

Bo opened her mouth to show him. "That tooth never came in," she said.

He raised his eyebrows. "Hmm," he said. "Maybe Doc will pull mine out and put it in your space!" Bo looked so horrified that Charlie soothed her. "Just joking," he said.

The man sitting next to Charlie said, "That's not a joke, you know. I read they could do that, put a tooth in an empty space. Like you take a plant out of one spot and put it in another." Charlie made a not-believing face, and the man said defiantly, "Read it in *Scientific American*."

A man from Eller's mine was telling the boys at the bar about a bad, bad toothache he got one winter while he was out on the trapline by himself.

"Got so bad I couldn't stand it anymore, so I got me a pliers. Wouldn't work. Couldn't get hold of that tooth. Got a chisel and hammer, and I started to work. First good whack, I passed out, came to, whacked at it again, passed out, did that two or three times. Woke up some time later, cold, the fire gone out, the whole bench covered with blood all gone thick and shiny like jelly, and the tooth lying in the middle of it. Built the fire, cleaned up the mess, washed my mouth with salt water, and had no more trouble."

Bo and the boys, their eyes huge and horrified, were each imagining taking a chisel with its sharp blade to one of their teeth. And then hammering the chisel!

A frowsy-looking man with wild stand-up hair and a striped apron over his overalls—Doc Larue—came out of the pantry where he was going to examine his patients. He beamed at Jack, pounded him on the back, and said, "Black Jack! Blood brother!"

Bo knew Black Jack was a nickname Jack had, but she didn't know anything about the blood business. She and the boys looked at Jack for an explanation, but Jack just laughed. "Old story," he told them.

"This the baby you and the Big Swede had at Ballard? Mean Millie's kid?" Doc asked.

Jack nodded. "Nearly growed up," he said.

"She the patient?" Doc asked.

They all nodded, so Doc put his hand on Bo's back to hustle her into the pantry.

"Don't get riled," he said over his shoulder to the waiting men. "She can't take long." Doc gestured for her to get up on a bar stool that was pushed up against the wall.

Buddy and Will tagged along behind Jack, and they all crowded into the little room.

"No tooth coming in yet," explained Jack. Doc looked in Bo's mouth.

"Big hole," said Doc. "Makes it hard to whistle."

"No, I can whistle good," Bo said, and she whistled to show him. Doc made a whadda-ya-know-about-that face. His breath smelled like whiskey. With his little mirror thing, Doc tapped the jaggedy ridges coming up after the last lost tooth.

"How long ago she lose this one?"

" 'Bout a week ago; new one popped up so fast

it looked like it'd been
pushing the old one out
of the way."

Doc tilted Bo's head
back so he could look
closely at the empty
hole on top. "And how
long's this one been
out?"

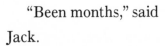

"Been months," said
Jack.

"Well, this one ain't never gonna show up," said
Doc Larue. "Gonna have a space there, right in
front, all your life. Someone shortchanged you when
they were passing out the grown-up teeth. Good
news, it will never give you a toothache."

"That's crazy," Will said enviously.

"Yeah," breathed Buddy.

Bo could tell they both wished they had a tooth
that didn't have a backup. They liked anything that
was different.

Bo didn't mind at all if a new tooth didn't grow
in. She liked the way she could make this interesting
sound through the space.

"I can do this," she said, showing off, and she made a spooky wind-blowing-through-the-willows sound through the space.

Jack raised his eyebrows at Doc. "What next?" he said.

"Not a girlie sort of girl," said Doc.

DOC STAYED ONLY two days before he was off to McGrath. All that week, the boys who came to visit told Doc Larue stories.

He was a very popular dentist, Doc. Even if he drank on the job and wasn't noticeably clean.

"People who make you laugh are much appreciated," Jack explained when he was going off to work. "And, by god, Doc would make a corpse laugh." Then he rushed out of the door before Bo could ask him what a corpse was.

CHAPTER FIFTEEN

A BIRTHDAY
AND A NAME

JACK CAME BACK from the post office one day, beaming.

"This," he said, waving a letter in front of their noses, "this is what we been waiting for a long while. Guess!" Bo and Graf stared at the letter, and suddenly Bo was sure she knew. "From Hank!"

Jack gave her an aren't-you-smart look. "Right the first time. Good old Hank, he's been wiring here and writing there, and he finally got the low-down on you, Graf." Jack took the letter out of the envelope and held it way out, as far as his arm would reach, so he could see it.

"Hank wrote to that mission where your auntie thought you were born, and this is what they told him." Jack looked down at them to be sure they were paying proper attention. "Your ma's name was Hazel, and your pa was Paul. You was born when they were up the Koyukuk trapping. February 12, 1926." Jack sat down and put the letter on the table. "I been figuring it out. Means you're older than we thought. Almost four and a half."

Jack could see Bo and Graf were waiting for more. "I know, I know," he said. "This letter don't tell you much, why your mom died, or when. Or anything about them. Don't say what they was like, what they could do, or all like that. What made them laugh.

"Someday maybe we'll run into someone from down there by Kaltag, find out something about your mom and dad," he said. "Got to talk to people who knew them to find out that kind of stuff. The important stuff."

That night when they were in bed, Graf asked, "What's your birthday?"

"Mine isn't a really one like yours," Bo said. "The papas just knew I was born in April, so Jack put a blindfold on me and Arvid put me in front of the April page in the calendar. And then I walked forward and my finger went on the tenth and that was my birthday."

Graf nodded, turned over on his side, and closed his eyes. Then he opened them suddenly. "How long till my birthday?"

NOT LONG AFTER they'd learned when Graf was born, Jack was sitting at the end of the kitchen table, filling out some papers and looking pretty cross about it, pulling faces and grumbling low in his chest.

Jack jerked his head at the chair next to him to tell Bo to sit down.

"Got to fill out these papers to get your school stuff," said Jack. As soon as Jack learned there was no school in Iditarod Creek, he'd asked Will and Buddy's father for the address of the Calvert School that the boys used. The papers had come on the last mail plane.

Bo watched for a few minutes as he shuffled papers around and looked more and more grumpy.

"You'll do your school right here with me in the morning, and what's left over you'll do with Arvid at night after I go to work," he said.

"Did you know there was no school here?" Bo asked.

"Never thought to ask, never gave it a thought. Surprise to me that there aren't more kids here."

"But how will you know how to teach school?"

"Done it already," said Jack. He laughed at the look of surprise on her face. "Taught one of the boys at the Circle diggings, an Albanian, to read and write one winter when things was slack. Back home, taught the girl I was going to marry and a young guy, kin to her."

"Did you have a school when you were little?"

"No, we didn't have no school. Fellow worked in the fields taught me. I was considerable older than you."

"Not Mama Nancy?"

"No, she never had no schooling. But this fellow, Tandy, he didn't learn to read till he was grown—learned from a friend—and then he taught me at night after he was finished working. It goes from one hand to another, like. I got to pass it on, and someday maybe you'll have to pass it on."

"Do you like teaching?"

Jack's face went smooth like it did when he was thinking something nice.

"I do. I like that look people get when they're catching on to something."

Jack leaned back in his chair. "So we'll teach you with all this Calvert stuff and then you can help Graf out."

"I think he already knows how to read," said Bo.

"Well, I don't think so," said Jack with a smile.

"Yes, he knows all the names on the cans."

"Does he?" said Jack, his eyebrows raised in surprise. He thought a second. "Probably because of the pictures."

He wrote *peaches* on a piece of paper and then he went to the door. Graf was outside in the sawdust by the woodpile, building a house with pieces of the lumber Arvid had thrown out after he made the shelves and table.

"Come 'ere, Graf," Jack said. He showed the paper to him.

"Know this word, Graf?"

"Peaches," said Graf. Bo looked sideways at Jack, an I-told-you look.

Jack frowned and wrote another word. *Milk.*

"Milk," said Graf.

"Some are like that," said Jack, as if he wasn't surprised. But his face looked as if he had never heard of such a thing before.

Jack sat back down and picked up one of the papers on the table.

"Here's the thing. You got to have a name."

Bo looked shocked. "I have a name. You gave me Bo, and Papa gave me Marta. I have two names."

"Well, yeah, but you need a last name, too. You know, like Jack Jackson and Arvid Ivorsen. A first name and a last name. Like us."

"Well, everybody doesn't have a last name. Lots of Eskimos don't have a last name." Bo wasn't fond of change.

"No, don't seem necessary until you got to fill out these blanking papers. I've seen plenty people had to think of one when the time came to fill out some papers. Couldn't leave the last name place empty."

"And Graf?"

"Him too," said Jack. "You heard the letter. His pa didn't have no last name." Jack bounced his pencil *rat-a-tat* on the paper, thinking.

"Where I come from, lots of people didn't have a last name of their own. Just named for the man they worked for." Jack's eyes squinched up. "Kind of like branding cattle," he said. "Jackson was the man owned the place where my mama was born. All of them worked there on his place was called Jackson for a last name."

Jack's face was still a moment, and then he smiled and tipped her chin up with his big finger. "So. What kind of last name would you like?" he said brightly.

"Can't we have your last names? Marta Jackson and Ivorsen?"

"S'posed to have just one last name."

"Couldn't we put them together?"

Jack smiled his tucked-in smile that dimpled both cheeks.

"Jacksonivorsen. Ivorsenjackson. Take you a month to say it, wouldn't it?"

Graf came into the kitchen, sat down on the other side of Jack, and watched them with his chin resting on the table.

Jack wrote down one name, studied it, and crossed it out; wrote a dozen more, scowling at the paper.

Jack suddenly smiled, looking pleased with himself. "Here's an idea just come to me. Could maybe name you for the place you was born. Or maybe the river. You was born on the Yukon, Graf on the Koyukuk."

"No," said Bo, frowning. "We like *your* names."

Jack could see he wasn't going to sell that idea, so he went back to his paper. "Ivorsen Jackson," he muttered darkly.

"Were you born on a river?" Bo asked.

"Mississippi," said Jack, not looking up.

Bo looked startled and darted her eyes at Graf. "We don't like river names," she said decidedly.

Bo watched Jack scribble this name and that on his paper.

"Your names both sound the same at the end," said Bo.

"They do," said Jack. "Spelled different. Swede way with an *e* and my way with an *o*."

He rubbed his head. "Maybe just use the first parts. Like Ivorjack or Jackivor. Or use one *son* for both, like Ivorjackson or Jackivorsen. Marta and Grafton Ivorjackson. Marta and Grafton Jackivorsen.

"Which one? Jack first, Ivor first?"

He looked at Graf. Graf just shook his head. They could see he wasn't very interested.

"Well, leave it be. Let's see what the Swede comes up with."

When Arvid came in from his shift, they showed him what they'd been thinking of.

Arvid said the two names over and over, as if he were tasting something.

"See, if you say Ivorjackson your mouth has to work too hard. But if you say Jackivorsen, it just slips out nice and easy."

They all tried it, and it was true. "But if you leave the end off, and it's Jackivor or Ivorjack, that's nicer and shorter." He practiced both for a second, then decided. "No, it's smoother with *Jack* first."

"So?" said Jack. "Marta and Grafton Jackivor?"

Graf and Bo said "Jackivor" over and over, until they got silly and fell in a heap laughing.

Jack shrugged on his jacket and headed out the door to work muttering, "Jackivor, Jackivor. Got to get used to it," he said.

Arvid wrote their new name on a piece of paper.

"Now you practice writing this, Bo. Marta Jackivor. That's your whole name."

And then he wrote *Grafton Jackivor*. "And you can practice that, Graf."

Bo practiced and prac-
ticed the new name, and
when she looked up,
she saw that Graf was
practicing his, too, holding the pencil all crazy.

But his writing was good.

Though he'd never written a thing before.

CHAPTER SIXTEEN

THE DEACON

B O AND GRAF and Arvid had just gotten back from the swing and were settling down to a game of checkers before they went to bed. Bo told Arvid about a chunky little man who'd come on the mail plane.

"Buddy said he was a preacher, come to visit Miz Eller."

"Oh?" Arvid said.

"See, he came once before, and Miz Eller said all the Eller men had to go to a prayer meeting, and she put up a sign in the store. But Buddy and Will said old man Eller stood up to her, said he wasn't going to tell his men they had to go to any prayer meeting. And Will and Buddy's mom and dad had a row about it. And just the Mizzes ended up going to the prayer meeting. What's a preacher, and what's a prayer meeting?"

Arvid tipped his chair back and laughed long and hard. "That Miz Eller," he finally said. "There's no end to the things she thinks of, is there?"

"Well, what's a prayer meeting?"

"Beats me," said Arvid. "Let's play checkers."

JUST WHEN THEY'D FINISHED that game and another, and Bo and Graf were in their pajamas, ready for bed, someone knocked on the door.

When Bo opened the door, there was the man she'd been talking about. She darted a startled look at Arvid, who didn't look at all surprised to find the preacher man on their doorstep.

The preacher looked surprised, though—people usually did when they saw how big the papas were. "I'm Deacon Mitchell," the man said, looking up at Arvid and mopping his face with a white handkerchief.

Arvid bent a bit and shook the man's hand. "Arvid Ivorsen," he said, smiling sweetly, his special full-of-the-devil smile. He waved his big hand at the children. "And this here is Bo and Graf."

Arvid raised his eyebrows. "What can we do for you, Deacon?"

The preacher shifted from one foot to the other and cleared his throat as if he was getting ready to give a speech.

"Miz Eller, who is concerned about the spiritual welfare of the people of Iditarod Creek—a place that is virtually godless—has called to my attention the very odd fact that you have in your care two small children. Of irregular parentage."

"True, true," Arvid said and waved his hand again. "Here they stand."

The preacher made a stern face. "May I ask if they are baptized?"

"No, best not ask," Arvid said pleasantly. "Our kids is heathens, pure and simple." He leaned forward as if he were telling a secret. "Been speaking Eskimo since they were born. I figure myself that they're possessed, and I don't mess with it at all. And they can swear in several languages." Arvid made a proud face. "Do you a treat to hear them carry on."

He tipped his head at Bo and Graf. "Go ahead," he told them. "Swear some in Eskimo. Preacher wants to hear you."

The fat man pulled his handkerchief out again, wiped his forehead some more, and scuttled out of the open door.

"Tell Miz Eller we appreciate her concern," Arvid called after him.

Arvid shut the door, and Bo and Graf watched him, astonished, as he laughed so hard he finally fell in a heap on the couch.

"Oh, oh," he moaned, "what a shame Jack missed that!"

CHAPTER SEVENTEEN

DOUGHNUTS

ON THE 29TH of June, it snowed.

Jack and Arvid said they'd known it to snow in the summer plenty of times. Of course the snow melted after an hour or so, and the next day it was hot, miserably hot, ninety degrees—a hundred degrees on the thermometer in the sun. Jack and Arvid had seen it that hot in the summer plenty of times too.

"Think of it," Arvid said. "Coldest day last winter was some sixty below. Today it's almost a hundred and fifty degrees warmer."

Arvid hated the heat. He turned bright red, sweat poured down his face, and his clothes got wet through. Jack didn't even notice the heat. He couldn't turn red like Arvid, and he didn't sweat, either.

"Consider where I grew up," he said. "This here is dry heat, not air so wet you could eat it with a spoon. Humidity. That's the thing gets to you."

The next day Jack started his doughnuts. "Wouldn't be Fourth of July if I didn't make doughnuts," he said.

But he and Bo didn't have to make them all by themselves this year. Carmen and Emma said they'd help too. Jack was very happy about that.

"I was just thinking I'd bit off more than I could chew," he told them. "In Ballard Creek we made four hundred, but we'll need twice that many here. Lot more people here." He rolled his eyes, just thinking about it. "You girls are going to save my life!"

"Nothing to it," said Emma cheerfully.

So Jack mixed a huge batch in his biggest bowl and after the dough rose, Bo and Emma and Carmen rolled it out and started cutting. Jack borrowed a big piece of plywood from Hardy, and they set it up on sawhorses in the front room. That's where they put the doughnuts to rise after they were cut out.

It was very crowded with that big board in there, and Bo and Graf had to edge around it if they needed to go in the front room. When the doughnuts were puffed up just the way Jack wanted—almost light enough to float away—they took turns frying them.

Carmen took the first turn after Jack showed her just how to do it. When they were brown on both sides, she lifted them out of the oil and onto a big towel. That was so some of the oil would soak into the towel. "No excuse for greasy doughnuts," Jack said.

Bo's job was to toss each doughnut around in a bowl of sugar, and then she and Graf would carefully put them all into the burlap bag they'd borrowed from Sidney at the store. But somehow the sugar got all over Bo's overalls and on her face and on the floor, and Graf was pretty well sugared too. And it crunched under their feet, which was annoying.

When Will and Buddy came to the door to see if Bo and Graf could come out, they stared astounded at the piles of doughnuts Bo was busy sugaring.

"Well, don't just stand there," Jack said. "Try them out!"

So Buddy and Will started in. "I'll bet I could eat a hundred," said Will.

But he didn't last long. He was so stuffed with doughnuts after a dozen or so that he had to quit. Buddy didn't eat as many as Will, but he put two in his overall pockets. "For later," he said.

"Now, here's your job," said Jack, who'd just thought of how the boys could make themselves useful. "Put this bag in the wagon and take them to Sidney," he said. "We want the doughnuts for the Fourth of July fresh as the day they were fried."

Everyone had a freezer hole for their meat. If you dug down far enough to permafrost where the ground never thawed, everything down there would stay frozen.

Jack said that was one of the most convenient things about living in the far north.

Sidney would put the doughnuts down in the hole, and the doughnuts would freeze just like the meat did.

After Buddy and Will hauled off the last hundred to Sidney's, Carmen and Emma were red-faced from the heat in the kitchen and looked pretty bedraggled.

Jack blew out his cheeks. *Whew.*

"Got to do this all over again tomorrow," he groaned. "And then once again."

After the first day, no one even wanted to try the doughnuts. And by the time they'd made eight hundred of them, Emma said she'd sworn off doughnuts forever, and she hoped Tom would never think of asking her ever to make doughnuts for him.

CHAPTER EIGHTEEN

FOURTH OF JULY

THE WEATHER WAS BEAUTIFUL for the Fourth.
It always was. Bo thought there must be some
sort of rule about it.

Best of all, the dredges were silent. It was quiet,
so quiet. All the mines were closed, and Arvid and
Jack had the whole day off, like everyone in all of
the mining camps around Iditarod Creek. The
Fourth of July was the most important holiday in
the year.

Bo and Graf were jittering around, half wild,

impatient for the papas to eat breakfast, clean up, get dressed.

"We'll be right on time." Arvid laughed down at them. "You'll see!"

Stig and Eero came by to see if they were ready. They could talk about nothing but the arm-wrestling contests. All the men for miles around had been talking about wrestling for weeks.

There was a muscle man at the Kilbourne dredge who was big on bodybuilding. He worked out with dumbbells all the time and was really skookum. They had figured Jack and Arvid would be his biggest competition, until Arvid hurt his arm at the dredge. It wasn't cured up yet, so he wouldn't be doing any wrestling.

"It's up to you, Jack!"

Stig felt Jack's arm, and Jack pumped it up with a braggy face to show him that it was in good shape.

"You'll do," said Stig.

Buddy and Will popped their heads in the door, but they were too impatient to wait. "See you down there!"

IDITAROD CREEK was a shockingly different town on the Fourth of July.

They could hear the hullabaloo of the crowd when they came out of the house. Bo and Graf darted frightened looks up at the papas.

"Just ready for a good time," Arvid reassured them. "Blowin' off a little steam."

When they could see the huge mob of miners, Bo and Graf clutched the papas' hands. They'd never seen so many men all together in their lives.

Every square inch around the hotel and the store was full of men, loud and boisterous, calling out to one another.

Bo looked up at Jack in dismay. "We didn't make enough doughnuts!"

"No," Jack said with a big laugh. "You can never make enough, but it'll have to do!"

Sidney had dumped all the doughnuts into four big washtubs, and the men were already helping themselves.

When they saw Jack, they cheered "hip, hip hooray!" to thank him for the doughnuts. Bo and Graf looked at each other, proud.

A big red, white, and blue banner was stretched

across the front of the hotel. FOURTH OF JULY IN IDITAROD CREEK 1930 it said in the fancy kind of letters that Bo liked so much.

The contests were just starting, so they were right on time, like Arvid said. Not the same contests they'd had in Ballard, because most of those had been for kids. These contests were a lot noisier and a lot rougher.

Yoshihiro and Haruto were the marshals. Marshals, Jack said, were to be sure that no one cheated. They were standing very tall, and Bo could see from their faces that they liked being the marshals very much.

The tobacco-spitting contest was first. The men lined up at the starting line, chewing and chewing their hunks of tobacco, the muscles of their jaws clenching and twisting, getting the tobacco juicy enough. When Yoshihiro blew the whistle, the men pushed out their lips and thin brown jets of tobacco juice shot out. A long way! Bo and Graf were impressed.

Bo didn't know the man who won, but he was from the Eller dredge, and his friends lifted him on their shoulders and carried him around while the men from the other dredges booed and shook their fists at them.

They were so loud and crazy even Bo hid behind the papas, like Graf always did when it was noisy.

Jack entered the wood-splitting contest, but he didn't come close to being the fastest.

"You can be big, or you can be fast," Arvid told them. "But you can't be both."

The wheelbarrow race was next, and Jack and Arvid were itching to have a try. The men pushing the wheelbarrow would be blindfolded, and the men sitting in the wheelbarrow would tell them which way to go.

"Go sit in front of the hotel," Arvid told Bo and Graf. "You might get trampled."

Then Jack loaded Eero in his wheelbarrow and Arvid took Stig, and they waited at the starting line with dozens of other men.

The path to the finish line was twisted, with curves and sharp turns. The wheelbarrows careened

all over the streets, tipping and spilling the passen-
gers, getting stuck and bashing into one another.

It was a terrible brawl, and the crowd was hoarse
from screaming.

When it was over, Jack and Arvid tore off their
blindfolds and said it wasn't *their* fault that they

were going crooked—it was Eero's and Stig's fault because they couldn't give good instructions.

And Eero and Stig said Jack and Arvid were hopeless at following simple directions and didn't know their left from their right.

It looked like the most fun thing in the world, and Bo wanted to try it. Tomorrow they'd borrow Hardy's wheelbarrow.

Maybe they'd try the spitting, too.

There were more games—footraces and three-legged races and burlap bag races. Some were so crazy Bo couldn't imagine how they'd thought them all up—mumblety-peg with jackknives and who could stand the longest on a greased log. And even crazier, a contest where they had to climb up a greased pole.

After all those were finished, Bo tugged Graf's arm. "Look," she said and pointed to the washtubs that had held the doughnuts. They were empty.

At last it was time for the arm wrestling. It was easy to tell this was the thing everyone had been waiting for, because the whole huge pack of men roared with excitement when Hardy called for all the contestants.

In the middle of the street, there was a big upright log about waist high, with a bench on either side for each wrestler to sit on. Each man planted his right elbow in the middle of the log, and they clasped hands while the crowd chanted, "Down, down, down."

Haruto held up his hand for silence, and when the crowd was quiet, he gave a blast on the whistle—and they were off. The two men grunted and strained, each trying to pull the other's arm down on the log. The winner would go another round with someone else and on and on, until finally there were only two left.

Bo and Graf were very pleased that their Maggie beat two men before she went down.

The last two left undefeated, as everyone had expected, were Jack and the guy from the Kilbourne dredge.

Bo was interested to see that the Kilbourne man's hair was slicked down some way and neatly parted right down the middle. She'd seen men like that in magazines.

"That's why his nickname is Dapper Dan," Eero said. "*Dapper* means *fancy*."

When the fancy guy took off his shirt, Bo and Graf stared at the ripples and bulges all over his body. It looked as if there were snakes under his skin.

Dapper Dan looked very pleased with himself.

All those hundreds of men stood in a circle around Jack and Dapper Dan, carrying on something awful.

It was so loud Bo glanced anxiously at Graf because he hated noise so much. But Graf wasn't hiding behind Arvid's legs—he looked fascinated. Maybe he was getting used to all the hoorah.

But when the men who wanted Jack to win began chanting, "Black Jack! Black Jack!" over and over, Arvid had to pick Graf up. The noise was deafening.

Bo got so excited she started yelling "Black Jack!" too.

The men from Kilbourne started yelling, "Dan! Dan! He's our man!" to drown out the Black Jack men.

Bo felt very cross with them.

Back and forth, slowly, Jack's arm strained, Dan's arm strained, almost but never quite touching the log. Dapper Dan was sweating, and veins were popping out on his head. His hair was not stuck down to his head anymore, or parted in the middle, but falling in his eyes.

Then for what seemed like a long, long time, their arms stayed upright, trembling, neither able to move the other.

Then Jack suddenly took Dapper Dan's arm down with a whack, and the crowd went mad.

Jack beamed, his teeth flashing white. He pounded enthusiastically on Dan's back and shook his hand ferociously. Bo thought it looked as if Jack had forgotten who was the winner.

But Arvid said Jack was pleased that the Kilbourne man had been so hard to beat. It was more fun that way, Arvid said.

Some of the men picked Jack up, arms and legs, and tried to carry him around, but he was so big they began to laugh and had to put him down. So they thumped him on the back some more and shook his hand up and down like a pump, beaming like crazies.

LATER THERE WAS a wonderful show.

Some boys from the Willard dredge put on a play, dressed up like ladies. Everyone screamed with laughter as they walked around in a silly way with their painted cheeks and red lips. And talked in high voices.

There was lots more: a magic show, a lot of little bands, a trumpet solo that Graf really liked, and Little Jill on the harmonica. Sadie and Carmen dressed up like men with round black hats and mustaches and canes and did a funny dance, and one man played a washboard—a *washboard*!

And finally, two accordions played together so people could dance.

The men had to dance with one another, mostly, because there were hardly any women—just the good-time girls and Emma and Paulie and Nita, and Louise who cooked at their dredge, and Maggie.

None of the Mizzes came to the Fourth of July.

Will and Buddy said every year their ma told them they couldn't go because there were too many rough men and unsuitable people.

"She says that every year until our pa roars at her and says he's tired of her stuck-up ways," Will said.

"And then he gets drunk," Buddy said with satisfaction.

Bo danced every dance, but Will and Buddy wouldn't dance at all, just folded their arms across their chests and gave her a disgusted look when she asked.

"Look, Arvid," Bo said. "Paulie can dance like anything!"

Arvid was not surprised. "Don't have to see to dance," he said.

WHEN THEY WERE finally tucked into their beds that night, Bo sighed with satisfaction.

"We finally got to see all the Charlies. Scotch Charlie and Charlie One-Eye. But I thought that meant he had one eye in the middle of his head, not just a patch over one eye. And—" She looked blank for a moment.

"Skookum Charlie was wrestling," said Graf.

"Oh, yes," said Bo. "And the Charlie like an Indian, with the band around his head and the feather."

"Cherokee Charlie," said Graf.

"And Little Charlie. He wasn't very little, was

he? And we already knew Charlie the Tram and Dago Charlie and Charlie Hootch."

"Good-Time Charlie, too," said Graf. "He came to the house once, remember."

Bo said them under her breath and counted on her fingers. "Nine!" She turned over and closed her eyes. "And Jack won the wrestling."

CHAPTER NINETEEN

AUGUST

ONE DAY WHEN Bo and Graf went to visit Nita and Paulie, Nita stuck her head out from the little shed by her house. She was holding a tin lard can by the handle, and she waved it at them. "We're going berry picking, me and Paulie," Nita said joyfully. "You better come, too."

Bo looked at the tailing piles all around them. "Where are the berries, Nita?"

Nita laughed. "Not here, for sure. We go out on the tundra near Bonanza City. Charlie the Tram takes us when he is going out there, lets us off to pick, and gets us on his way back. Right now, he says, the berries are perfect!"

"Go home, see if Jack will let you come," Nita ordered. "Meet us at the tram!"

BO HADN'T KNOWN how much she missed the tundra at Ballard until she smelled the Labrador tea and the dirty-socks stench of the high-bush cranberries.

And she was nearly astounded at the brightness all around her; she had grown so used to the drab tailing piles in Iditarod Creek. Scarlet blueberry leaves, fuchsia and burnt orange Labrador tea, yellow spongy moss, red lichens and gray lichens with ruffled edges clinging to the rocks, and pink grass, peony pink, bending and swaying in the tiniest breeze.

Paulie's delicate fingers could find the berries so easily, it was hard to believe she couldn't see them. Bo knelt by Paulie and bent her head low to look closely at the tundra by her knees.

"It's like a little world down here, Paulie. A tiny woods full of tiny strange trees and flowers. What would it be like to be that spider taking a walk through the tall lichen trees, stopping to look at the red flowers? Their stems are thin, like a stiff thread, and the flowers are the size of beads. Shiny red beads. And here by your boot, there's a tiny yellow spider—even his legs are yellow. He's yellow all over, and he's zigzagging through the lichen and moss."

Bo picked something from the tundra for Paulie to admire. "Hold out your hand," she said. "Here are tiny, tiny white mushrooms only as big as a pinhead."

It didn't matter that Paulie couldn't see with her eyes. She saw with something else, and Bo was sure from Paulie's lovely smile that she was seeing that tiny world in her head.

AFTER LUNCH, NITA SAID, "We find mouse food now."

She showed them how to find the little mounds where the voles had hidden their cache of roots.

"Yup'ik people love these roots boiled. I'll make some for you."

When she found a little bulge, she cut it open carefully with her knife, took the roots stashed there, and put them in her basket.

Bo looked at Nita unhappily. To be taking what the little vole had so patiently gathered!

But Nita smiled when she saw Bo's face.

"In the Yup'ik way, we share with the animals. Look what we do." Nita took pieces of dried fish and meat from her basket and put them into the empty hole. Then she covered it over the way the vole had done. "That way the vole won't starve in the winter. I think maybe he'll be happy to find fish and meat. That's better than roots."

The Yup'ik, Nita said, would never take something without paying for it.

WHEN IT WAS RAINING, which it did a lot in August, they usually went to Eero and Stig's or to the hotel, where Bo and Graf and Will read magazines and Buddy played pinochle with old Henry.

This rainy day, they'd visited Eero and Stig first. The boys worked on their knots with Eero, and Bo told Stig one of her long letters to Ballard Creek. It took a long time for the mail to come to Iditarod Creek, so they'd only had one letter from Ballard. But Jack said that soon the mail would catch up with them and they'd get a lot of letters all at once. Bo could hardly wait for that to happen.

When she finally finished her letter, Bo said good-bye and left the boys there. She was eager to get to the hotel, because she knew Hardy had two new records which she'd only heard a few times.

She liked "Tiptoe Through the Tulips" the best. Hardy had to tell her what tulips were, because she'd thought it was "two lips," which didn't make sense.

After she'd played that record two times, she looked for another, one of her favorite opera records that Tomas had played for her in Ballard Creek. Caruso.

But as soon as she put it on the gramophone, everybody started to make a fuss and groan. "No opera!"

Hardy told them to let her be, but she felt bad playing something nobody liked. So she took the record off the turntable.

Hardy glared at all the old-timers who'd complained to Bo, and then he pulled all the Caruso records off the shelf and piled them in her arms.

When she got home, Jack raised his eyebrows when he saw all the records she
was holding.

"Hardy said I could have all
the Caruso records I wanted because
nobody else liked them. Just like
Ballard. Nobody there liked Caruso
either. Except Tomas."

She put the records on the shelf
with the others and then counted
them. "Now we have seventeen altogether. You want
to hear my best Caruso one, 'La Donna È Mobile'?"

Jack smiled bravely. "You bet," he said.

ONE GRAY DAY, Charlie the Tram came from
Bonanza City with a huge box in one of his tram
wagons.

As soon as Buddy and Will caught sight of the
big box, they left Bo and Graf sitting on the boardwalk and tore off to the freight barn.

It wasn't long before they were back, breathless.
Buddy leaned forward, his hands on his knees, gasp-
ing for breath.

"It's a piano in there," Will said. "For Eller! Came all the way from *Seattle*."

Buddy could talk now. "On the ocean, on the train to Fairbanks, from Fairbanks to Nenana, from Nenana on the sternwheeler and up the Innoko and Iditarod. And still in one piece, Charlie said."

"What's a piano?" asked Bo.

"Used to be one in the old dance hall," said Will. "Got busted up in a fight. I really liked to listen to it."

In a while, one of Eller's men brought the Cat from Eller's mine, and together with Charlie, they loaded the box on the go-devil.

Buddy and Will and Bo and Graf watched the piano box as the Cat hauled it away slowly, slowly, over the tailing piles to Eller's house.

"That's the biggest box I ever saw," said Buddy.

After that, they could often hear scraps of piano music from all the way across town if the wind was blowing the right way. Then Buddy and Will and Graf and Bo would sneak around the Eller house to listen up close. Mostly because Will was crazy about pianos.

Even if it was horrible Miz Eller playing, they liked to listen. She didn't do any of the songs they knew from the gramophone at Hardy's hotel or the records they had in Ballard. They were serious sort of songs with a lot of thumping parts.

They all wished they could have a turn at that piano.

CHAPTER TWENTY

WINTER COMING

NITA SEWED FUR MITTS and mukluks and parkas for a living. She was the only one in Iditarod Creek who did skin sewing, so she was always at it, her worktable spread with cut-out fur pieces and bars of soap stuck full of needles. She said soap made the needles more slippery.

Jack needed a new pair of mukluks for winter. He'd had Nita measure his big feet, and he told her to make a pair for Arvid too, while she was at it. When Nita sent a note to tell Jack his boots were ready, Jack sent Bo down to Nita's with the money tied in a handkerchief.

Nita wrapped up the new boots for Bo. They were beautiful, with a green knitted top, an appliquéd band of black fur diamonds and squares, and bright green ties with big yarn pompoms.

"Tell him they don't fit good, bring them right back," said Nita. She patted the package. "But I know they'll fit just right. I started next pair for Arvid, got the tops finished already. Tell him he'll get them soon."

She poured Bo some tea and put a box of cookies on the table.

Bo had never eaten a store cookie. They were golden and folded into little pillows, with a brown sort of jam inside.

"That's Fig Newtons. Try one," said Nita. "Too busy sewing, I'm lazy to bake. Got these from Sidney's store, but they cost too much."

Bo liked the way the Fig Newtons were so perfectly lined up in the box, tight against one another. But she didn't like the way they tasted.

Nita dipped hers in her tea. "I got someone to talk Yup'ik with now!" she announced cheerily.

Bo put her cookie down and looked at Nita.

"This one boy, never saw him before, he comes to visit. Knocks on the door real quiet. Said he heard I talked his language."

"Oh!" said Bo. "That's the boy everyone keeps telling us about. But we never saw him. Why does he speak Eskimo?"

"His mother was Yup'ik from on the Kuskokwim. She died, and he came here with his father, little while back. His father's working at the Willard dredge. His father's not Yup'ik. Something from far away. I forget what.

"This boy was so glad to talk with me. Didn't forget much, and pretty soon he's just talking fast. Me too. Slow and then faster. Like when you're pouring ketchup—at first it's slow, and then all of a sudden, it rushes out. We were both happy to be talking the right way again."

"Me and Graf, we talk Eskimo together so we don't forget. Arvid says keep it up because it's easy to lose a language. He can't talk Swede anymore."

Paulie came into the kitchen and sat at the table with them. "You should have heard that boy and Mama, just talking away. I don't know what they're saying."

"Not your fault," said Nita. "My fault. I don't talk Eskimo to you."

"You thought I'd get confused," Paulie said comfortingly.

Nita looked sorry. "Should've," she said.

"His name is Renzo," said Paulie. "He's older than you, maybe ten. Got no brothers or sisters. Not very big, up to my chin only." She looked at the ceiling. "Skinny," she said.

"How can you tell if someone's skinny?" asked Bo.

Paulie made a motion with her hands. "The way their clothes sound," she said. "Heavy people, their clothes don't slide around so much or something. And he was real polite."

"Yup'ik people is always polite," said Nita.

BO DIDN'T LIKE that gray, in-between, colorless time before the snow came. At Ballard, the geese and

ducks and cranes with their long, long legs were flying south. But here at Iditarod Creek, there were no
birds to say good-bye to.

It was almost freeze-up time, and dredge mining
was finished for the season. The bosses sent all their
gold to Fairbanks and paid the men off.

"Twenty years ago when all the gold was on the
tram going to Fairbanks, two fellas robbed the
tram," Arvid told Bo and Graf.

"All the gold, Papa?" Bo asked, horrified.

"Every bit," said Arvid. "But they caught them
and got half of it back. The rest they'd hid someplace on the tundra. Never found it. Every once in
a while, someone will take a notion he knows where
it is and go looking. No luck so far," Arvid said
cheerfully.

"Robbers," breathed Bo. She wondered what
other interesting things had happened in Iditarod
Creek before they came.

It was a strange feeling when the dredges shut
down. They had all said they'd never stop hating
the noise of the dredge, but they had. They'd stopped
noticing, almost forgot to complain about it.

Now there was quiet, no train-wreck noise. A

dozen times a day, Jack or Arvid would look at each other and say, "Can't get used to it."

But now they could hear the cold wind that seemed to have come to stay. It wasn't the quiet wind Bo had loved at Ballard that whispered and played in the trees. It was a mean, hell-raising wind, ripping at the loose sheet iron on the old buildings, rattling in the tailing piles, quarreling around corners.

Arvid tied the seats of their wonderful swing to the uprights where they'd be safe during the winter—couldn't bang around and get beat up.

A whole year's worth of hay for Charlie the Tram's horses came on the sternwheeler every summer. Charlie stored it all summer in a warehouse in Bonanza City, but in the fall before the tramline got snowed under, Charlie brought the hay to his barn in Iditarod Creek.

He'd also shipped in huge burlap bags of oats for their treats. His twelve good horses would have the winter off.

All the potatoes and onions and eggs for Iditarod Creek came on the last sternwheeler, too. They were stored underground in Hardy's root cellar.

By the time next summer came, the eggs would taste strange, but it happened slowly, so no one noticed very much.

Almost all the men from the mines left the country when the dredges shut down.

They went to Fairbanks to jump on the train, which took them to Seward to catch the last boats leaving for Seattle, and from there they'd go wherever they wanted. They'd visit their families, live a little high on the hog for a while after a summer of hard slogging.

They'd show off the money they'd made and always carried a few nuggets in their pockets just to make people's eyes pop.

It was a strange and lonesome place, Iditarod Creek, with most of the men gone. The boardwalks were empty, and there were not so many visitors.

But every year some of the men stayed—the ones who were in charge of getting the dredges ready for the winter or the ones who were to close up the mining camps. Some who stayed made money in the winter cutting wood or hauling freight from down on the Kuskokwim or from the mouth of the Yukon by dogsled or Cat.

Arvid and Jack were both blacksmiths by trade, and there was plenty of welding work for them in the winter.

And of course they'd stay the winter because Bo needed to start her schooling.

Now they were all together for dinner at night just like they'd been at Ballard Creek. It hadn't seemed bad when they were working shifts, and Arvid and Jack and Bo and Graf had all said many times that it all worked out fine.

But now that the papas were not on shifts, they could all see that things had been rushed and odd with only one papa home at a time.

It was going to be a wonderful winter with all of them home at the same time.

CHAPTER TWENTY-ONE

FIRST DAY OF SCHOOL

T HE BIG BOX from the Calvert company had come in August.

There was a strange picture on the box—a black sideways face of what looked like a curly-headed boy. Something about that boy made Bo uneasy.

Bo showed Stig the picture on the box, and Stig told them that was called a silhouette, the shadow of someone.

That's what it had seemed like to Bo. A shadow, not a real thing.

Bo and Graf begged Jack to open the box, but he wouldn't. "Things get scattered all over, you do that," he said. He shoved the box under the bed in Arvid's room and didn't bring it out again until it was time for the first day of school.

AT LAST IT WAS the day the Calvert people said they must begin.

Buddy and Will had been groaning for days, just thinking about it.

"All that boring stuff we got to read!" Buddy complained.

"And long division," said Will. "I can't stand long division."

Of course Bo was looking forward to school. The things she did with Jack and Arvid were usually fun and interesting.

"What about the boy at Willard dredge?" Bo asked. "Is he doing Calvert too?" They all shrugged their shoulders.

"He hasn't got a ma," said Will. They'd heard enough to know the boy's father wasn't the teacher type.

"And no house," said Buddy.

So school didn't sound like the kind of thing that boy would be doing.

The Calvert people had lists and lists of just when you must do something. Jack pinned the lists on the wall next to the map of the world. It made Bo feel rebellious to be bossed around like that.

"Well," said Bo, "they can't see us, and they don't know when we do stuff."

Jack slid his eyes sideways at her to show her that he wasn't impressed with that argument.

Jack put the boxes from Calvert on the table with a thump and slit the strings open with his pocket knife. He sorted out what was in the boxes: pencils and crayons and pads of paper with lines on them, two folded-up maps, and a lot of books— reading and science and history.

Bo and Graf pressed close to him and didn't even try to touch the things. They were so new and clean and uncomfortable looking. Everything had that Calvert boy on them, the maps and the books and the paper pads. Even the pencils—every single pencil.

Some of the books were for Jack and Arvid.

"These here are the learning guides," Jack said. "Tells us what to teach you and how to do it."

He put the pencils and crayons in two clean tin cans. Finally everything was on the table and sorted into piles.

Jack told them to sit down. He sharpened three of the pencils with his pocket knife and then he opened the big teacher's book. He flipped through its pages with his lips pursed and blew his cheeks out. Bo could see he was a bit nervous about this school business.

He unrolled a long paper with the alphabet on it. Each letter had a picture over it. It was just like the

one in the school in Ballard Creek, but with different pictures for some of the letters.

Jack put a can of corn at each end of the strip to keep it flat.

"This teacher's book here tells me what to have you do every day," Jack said. "Right now, I got to show you these letters, and you got to see that there are two kinds of letters. The ones on the left are the capital letters, and the ones on the right are the—" Jack looked in the book to see what they were called. "Lowercase letters," he read.

He pointed to the next page in the teacher's book.

"Now they say we got to count the letters."

Counting always made Bo feel anxious, because she kept skipping some. She began to falter after twenty-two, but under her voice was Graf's, and he was counting in his growly voice all the way to twenty-six. Without ever stopping. Jack sat very still and looked at Graf, his eyebrows raised so high that four straight lines appeared on his forehead. Graf looked back.

"Didn't know you could count that high," Jack said finally. Graf's face was deadpan.

"How far can you count?"

Graf shook his head and looked uncertain. He didn't know.

Jack bent his head back to his teaching manual and then he led Bo and Graf in reciting the alphabet in a singsong kind of way.

"Each letter makes a different sound," said Jack, "and here's how Tandy taught me. He's the one taught me to read. See, a cow don't say its name—it makes a certain sound. Its name is cow, but it says 'moo.' And *A* don't say 'a,' well, not all the time, but it makes another sound. Like the start of *apple*. That's why that picture's there. Every letter's got a picture. You remember the picture, you'll always know the sound of the letter."

"Oh," said Bo. That made sense.

Next Jack took out the alphabet book Bo was supposed to work in and showed her how she was to find the things that started with the *A* sound.

"Like this," said Jack. "Say just the first sound of *apple*."

"A, a, a!" they all said and then laughed uproariously because "a, a, a" sounded like a steam engine when it was just starting up. When they'd finished laughing, Jack relaxed a little and didn't look quite so serious.

After Bo had drawn a circle around all the things that started with *A*, she knelt on the chair and bent forward to study the letters on the strip.

"What I think," said Bo, "is that whoever made up these letters shouldn't have made them so much the same. How are you supposed to tell them apart?" She showed Jack the little *b* and the little *d*, and she showed him the *m* and *n*. "One hump and two humps," she said. "That's the only difference."

"Used to give me fits too," said Jack. "Used to write them all backwards at first."

In her book she was to trace over the dotted lines to copy the big *A* and the little *a*. Over and over, so it would stick in her head.

Graf looked at Jack expectantly, so Jack made a page of letters for Graf to trace as well.

Bo held her pencil the way they showed in the instruction book, but Graf grabbed his pencil in his fist like he always did. Jack showed Graf the picture, two fingers holding the pencil, thumb and forefinger, and then he held Graf's hand to show how he should write the new way.

But every time Jack looked up, Graf was back with the fist again. Jack sighed and gave up.

"Guess you'll get over it before you're grown," he said. "Never saw a grown person holding a pencil like that."

After they'd written the letters in their alphabet book, the teacher's book said they were to go to the counting chart. Bo worked on counting to thirty, and then she had a page with rabbits to count, and she had to write the numbers on some dotted lines. Jack made Graf some papers so he could work along with Bo.

She was very busy with one thing following the

other, and she had to sit down for all of it, so she was already getting wiggly. Sitting was not one of her best things.

"If I was you," she said to Graf in Eskimo, "I would go outside and play. Instead of sitting here."

Graf's green eyes roamed around while he considered what she'd said. Then he looked at her. "I like it," he said. "I like school."

When the alphabet and the numbers were finished, Jack had to read her a fairy tale from the Calvert book of stories. She must listen carefully so she could tell him the story back.

So Jack opened the book and read the first story, "Little Red Riding Hood." Graf heard it without expression, but Bo twisted and turned in her chair and looked unhappy.

When it was finished, Bo said, "Animals can't talk." She frowned. "And wolves don't eat people."

"Well," said Jack, "stories are not supposed to be real. They're ... unreal. Pretend. Imagination stuff."

Bo didn't look impressed.

Jack looked hopefully at Graf.

"*Was* silly," said Graf.

Jack gave him a sharp look. "I remember back when you didn't have any opinions." Jack straightened his shoulders and tried again. "The thing is," he said, "you got to know these stories because they're famous. All the kids in the world know them. Everyone does. That's a thing about education. Everyone has to know the same things. Or they wouldn't have nothing in common, like."

Bo squinted at Jack. "Did you like fairy tales when you were little?"

Jack let out a whoop of laughter. "Never heard one in my life!"

Bo was not amused. Jack looked at her stern face and compromised. "Well, don't tell it back to me—just draw a picture of it."

Bo thought that was a fine idea. Jack said it had better be a good picture because he had to send all Bo's work back to Calvert when she was done.

So Bo drew very carefully. To think of that Calvert boy seeing her picture! She and Graf both drew the part where the wolf was eating up Grandma.

That was their only favorite part of the story.

CHAPTER TWENTY-TWO

THE PACKAGE

BACK IN THE EARLY SUMMER, Bo and Graf had
been at the hotel, both squished up together in
one of the armchairs. They were almost mesmerized
by the pictures in a story in *National Geographic*
about snakes. Slim Carlson from Donal Sather's
mine came in, and he stopped by the chair when he
saw the looks on their faces.

"What's got you kids so interested?"

They showed him the pictures they'd been staring at. Huge snakes that took ten people to hold up,

stretched out. Snakes of every color. A shining green one with a wicked-looking forked tongue.

There was no such thing as a snake in Alaska. Nothing that lived in Alaska had fangs. Or poison! So of all the animals they'd ever heard of, snakes seemed the most shocking.

"Well, don't get any funny ideas about snakes," Slim said. "Most is just harmless. Silly people get scared of them."

"Have you seen a snake?"

"Seen a snake? Hundreds! Thousands! Got all kinds where I come from. Used to catch 'em and keep 'em for pets. Recognize you just like a dog, rush over to the side of the cage when you come in the room, tongue out, saying howdy."

"Aren't they scary?"

"Nah," Slim said. "Don't know why people always make such a blankety fuss over them. I've got no patience for them people. Don't even have any legs, snakes. Now, a crocodile or something could chase you, that's another proposition, but a snake ain't gonna run you down and ain't going to eat you."

"But what about those fangs?"

"Ain't gonna bite you neither, 'less you scare him. Besides, most snakes don't do nothing. Just mind their business and catch bugs and that."

"Did you *hold* one?"

"Well, I hope to *shout*. Lots of times. Like to look at them up close. People call them slimy. But they're dry as a bone and real pretty. Look like they're made of beads or something. Got nice patterns."

Bo and Graf blinked at Slim. Everything they thought about snakes was wrong.

"I wish we could see one," said Graf.

Slim laughed. "I'll bring you one when I come back in the spring."

AFTER THE SEASON ENDED and most of the boys had left Iditarod Creek, a month into winter, Jack sent them to the post office to get the mail.

Maggie gave Yoshihiro his mail, and then she gave Bo the papas' mail. Bo was putting it in the burlap sack Jack had given her when she saw that there was a little box with their mail, tied with thick string. Their names were on it! Bo and Graf!

"Maggie, who sent us this?" Bo asked.

Maggie looked at the writing on the box and

smiled. "From Slim," she said. "All the way from Oregon."

"Good to get a package," said Yoshihiro. "No such thing as bad package," and then he went out the door.

Bo couldn't wait till she got home to see what Slim had sent them. "Let's open it," she said. She borrowed scissors from Maggie and was so excited she just cut the string, didn't save it for Jack.

They pulled the top off the box and looked in. It was a toy snake.

"Probably he sent it because he was telling us all about snakes," Bo explained to Maggie. "Slim really likes snakes."

Bo was just about to take it out of the box when the toy snake suddenly moved, and with a quick twist, it was out of the box and on the table. It was alive! It was real!

Maggie screamed such a terrible scream that Bo's and Graf's hearts nearly stopped. She ran into the back room, still hollering. The snake froze, and for a minute Bo thought Maggie's scream had killed it.

Suddenly the door was flung open, and there was Yoshihiro again, looking horrified. Bo could tell

he'd heard Maggie screaming. He took in everything in a second—Maggie on the chair in the back
room, screaming her head off, the snake curled on
the table—and fast as a flash, he scooped the snake
into his hand and put it carefully back in the box.
Yoshihiro wasn't the least afraid of snakes.

He put the top on the box, and then he went in
back to deal with Maggie.

"Maggie, Maggie, just a little snake. Can't hurt
you. Just eats flies." He patted Maggie comfortingly
on the arm, but Maggie didn't get off the chair. She
still looked paralyzed. She'd stopped screaming, but
she was making little helpless squeaks.

Yoshihiro started to laugh, a high and funny
laugh, "He he he!" He tried to stop laughing, but
he'd start up again. "He he he he!"

Finally he quieted down and looked at Bo and
Graf. "Where snake come from?"

Bo told him about Slim and how they'd thought
it was a toy until it moved.

"It was cold, come in the mail like that in winter.
Come into hot room, and he's okay again. You not
afraid?"

Bo and Graf looked at him uncertainly. "Slim said not to be afraid of snakes."

"That good," said Yoshihiro.

Maggie was still making funny noises on the chair.

"Maggie, Maggie," Yoshihiro said. "Two big men you beat at wrestling—you strong woman. And here you screaming for a tiny snake."

"Put it away somewhere," Maggie said crossly. She came off the chair but stayed hiding in the back room.

"Put box in your jacket, keep it warm. Carry it careful," Yoshihiro told them. "It's good luck, snake, in Japan. Good to have in garden."

Bo put the rest of the mail in the burlap bag and gave it to Graf to carry. "I'll carry him," she said, and tucked him inside her parka.

Then she beamed at Graf. "Won't Jack and Arvid be surprised!"

CHAPTER TWENTY-THREE

CHARLIE HOOTCH

EVERY MORNING after the dishes were done and the floor mopped, Bo and Graf and Jack—and Arvid if he didn't have a welding job—sat down and rolled back the oilcloth to begin school.

Charlie Hootch was one of the miners who never left Iditarod Creek after cleanup. He always stayed through the winter. Charlie was a good carpenter, and Hardy never ran out of work for him—maybe building new storage shelves or putting in a closet. Little jobs like that.

And he stayed to keep his own business going, selling whiskey and kegs of homemade beer.

One morning Charlie came early, acting stiff, not like himself. After he'd admired their snake in its glass pickle jar and poured his coffee, Charlie pushed his cup aside, straightened up, and cleared his throat. He looked very serious.

"Jack, I'm wondering if I could learn to read along with your girl here. I'm some troubled that I never learned to read or write, and I sure would like to fix that."

Jack looked at the rolled-up magazine Charlie Hootch had sticking out of his pocket. Charlie shrugged his shoulder. "I just look at the pictures, figure out what I can."

Jack nodded. "Used to do the same, before I learned to read."

Bo and Graf looked back and forth between the two men, surprised. "Why can't you read?" Graf asked.

"Not everyone gets to go to school, you know," Jack answered for Charlie. "I wouldn't be able if Tandy didn't feel bad for me."

"How old was you?" asked Charlie Hootch.

" 'Bout sixteen, I think. Not too long before I come north."

"I'm thirty-four," said Charlie Hootch. "You figure that's too old?"

"Never too old," said Jack, smiling. "Learning gets easier when you get older."

Charlie Hootch made a doubtful face. "Don't know about that," he said. "Used to learn a song the first time I heard it. Now it takes me forever."

"Well, yeah," Jack said slowly. "That's true about remembering things, I guess. Like these kids learned Eskimo natural as breathing. I never learned more than a few words. Just don't have a place in my head for Eskimo words." He nodded, a little wistful. "Get older, things don't stick like they used to."

Jack looked happier all of a sudden. "What is easier when you're older is stuff that takes figuring. Like if you know how a steam engine works, it's easy to learn how a gas engine works. Don't have to remember, have to figure."

"Well, is reading a remembering thing or a figuring thing?" Charlie asked.

Jack thought for a moment. "Some of both, I think," he said. Then he laughed his deep, rumbling laugh. "Well, slow or fast, you can learn, Charlie, and high time, too. Me and Bo and Graf would be proud to have you here at our school."

Charlie Hootch's troubled face lit up suddenly. "Thanks, Jack," he said.

Bo leaned against Jack's big arm. She was proud that he'd made Charlie Hootch look like that, so joyful.

"Graf," Jack said, "while me and Bo are working on this reading, how about you start to teach Charlie the alphabet."

Both Charlie and Graf gave Jack a blank astonished stare.

"I'm only four and a half," said Graf.

"Don't see what that has to do with it," said Jack.

WHEN STIG and some others came in to drink coffee and found Graf busy at work teaching Charlie Hootch, Bo thought for sure they'd tease Charlie. But they didn't have anything funny to say at all.

Glenner Campbell said his teacher wasn't much

older than Graf. "Was my nephew, Homer, learned me to read before I left home."

Dave Blakker nodded. "My little sister taught me when she was still in grammar school." He smiled, remembering. "Strict with me, too. Kids make good teachers."

Frenchie told them what a hard time he'd had learning to read. He'd gone to the nuns' school in Montreal every day. "They used to smack me with the ruler when I made a mistake," he said.

But when he knew how to read and write a little, his dad took him out of school to go to work, so he'd never gotten really good at either one.

Charlie Hootch pointed his pencil at Frenchie. "Well, what are you waiting for?" he asked. "Got a chance to pick up some more schooling. No nuns to get after you, either."

Now that Charlie had started learning, he was pushing everyone else to try it, too.

CHAPTER TWENTY-FOUR

MEETING RENZO

I T TOOK LONGER for Nita to make Arvid's new mukluks than she'd said it would because she'd stopped to make a pair for the Yup'ik boy.

"I know how he is now," she said. "He don't like to take nothing. Always I tell him here's some soup, he says, 'I'm not hungry.' And you can see he's just bones. So I made him some good mukluks, nothing fancy, and I rubbed them with some dirt to make them look like they were used. So that way he would take them.

"But he said he got to work for them. Cut wood

for me. He won't take nothing without working for it. I said sure, I can use lots of wood cut up. Then he asked me if I'd keep the boots here for him till it snows. Didn't want to take them home. Said he didn't have anyplace to keep them. I just got a bad feeling about that."

Bo told Jack and Arvid at the supper table what Nita had said. Both of them put down their forks and looked searchingly at Bo.

"I heard about him," Arvid said to Jack. "Didn't know his dad stayed to do winter work on the dredge."

Arvid looked at Bo and Graf. "How old's this kid?"

Graf and Bo shook their heads. Didn't know.

Arvid and Jack asked around, but no one seemed to know much. Even Hardy, who usually knew everything, said he didn't know anything, really. Just didn't think much of the father.

WHEN NITA sent word that Arvid's mukluks were ready, Bo and Graf scampered down the tailing piles to Nita's house to pick them up.

That's when they finally saw the Yup'ik boy.

He was standing inside the fence, in the sawdust, splitting Nita's wood. He chopped like a grown man—fast and strong. But Bo was surprised to see how little he was. Thin, like Paulie said.

His hair was curly like Little Jill's, thick black curls over his ears, falling in his face. At first he acted like he didn't see them, but after a few minutes, he dropped the ax and came up to the fence. He smiled down shyly at them.

"Hey," he said.

Bo shook the boy's hand, and then Graf did, too.

"I'm Bo, and this is Grafton. But everyone calls him Graf."

"I'm Lorenzo," the boy said. "Lorenzo Donatelli. But everyone calls me Renzo."

He had a Yup'ik accent like Nita. Brown eyes, almost black.

"Nita told me about you," he said. "About your papas. You got adopted."

Bo nodded, surprised, because everyone said that he didn't talk.

His clothes were very dirty, and his leather boots were in terrible shape, but they had good strong bootlaces made of braided grass.

"Nita braids grass like that," Bo said. "Did she braid those laces for you?"

"No, my mom taught me how. She could make anything out of grass. You got a mom?"

Bo and Graf both shook their heads.

"Mine's dead, too," said Renzo.

"Your mom was Yup'ik, like Nita," said Bo.

"What was your mom?" asked Renzo.

"Me and Graf had different moms. His mom was Hazel from Kaltag. And my mom was Mean Millie. I don't know what she was. Nobody ever said."

"Do you remember her?"

"No, neither of us do. You remember your mom?"

Renzo's face went still. "Yeah," he said.

Bo and Graf had promised Jack they'd come right back, so they said good-bye to the boy and got the mukluks from Nita.

As they ran back home, they thought of a dozen questions they might have asked him.

CHAPTER TWENTY-FIVE

FOUR MORE

THE CALVERT COURSE sent books for Bo that were about a boy and a girl and their dog. Dick and Jane and Spot. And there were Sally and Puff, a baby and a cat.

There was also a mother who wore dresses and funny shoes with high, skinny heels. And a father who wore an outfit with buttons. A suit, Jack said.

Not only were the people in the book strangely dressed and strange looking, their talk was embarrassing.

"This is not a good book," Bo said. " 'Oh oh oh!

See Spot. See Spot run.' What kind of talk is that?"
She gave Jack a beseeching look.

Jack pursed his lips and thought a minute.

"I see your point," he said.

"Here, then, we'll just practice with these," and
he showed her the pack of cards that came with the
Dick and Jane books. One word on each card.

Bo and Graf learned those words in no time, and
then Jack was hard-pressed to know what to do
about reading.

Stig said nothing to worry about, you could learn
reading any old place. He'd learned to read from the
grain bags at his farm in Finland, and Zeke said
he'd learned from the Bible, and one of the men had
learned from cans, just like Graf.

"Now that I think on it," Jack said, "I learned to
read from an old almanac, so beat up I could hardly
make out the letters."

So Jack went through a *National Geographic*
and copied down all the words that seemed like they
happened a lot and made cards out of them. And
that was what Bo used for reading, along with the
old magazines Hardy had saved, the Sears catalog,
and anything else they could find.

STIG AND EERO came every day to help Graf and Charlie Hootch, and in a few more days, Glenner Campbell from Eller's mine and Frenchie asked to come to school too. And a few days after that, Dago Charlie came. He could read, but he couldn't write at all.

So Jack and Arvid had five more students than they'd thought they would when they first ordered the Calvert course.

Stig was teaching them about the night sky. There were no trees to block their view, so the sky looked way bigger than it had in Ballard. When it was too cold to be cloudy, when it was forty or fifty below, Bo and Graf liked to lie outdoors all bundled in their winter clothes and look up at the northern lights and the stars. Stig had given them a book of the constellations, and they'd find them every night, just where the book said.

The sky had a map—just like the world.

Stig and Eero weren't the only ones who helped teach. Yoshihiro and Haruto came, too. They were both good at teaching arithmetic, which was the same in Japan as Alaska. And now that Bo and Graf

had a snake, Yoshihiro was teaching everyone about reptiles, which was something he knew a lot about.

Even Carmen came sometimes.

Carmen was really strict about writing: "You have to start at the top! Pull the pencil down, not up!" They were all a little scared of her.

Everything Bo and Graf studied set off a dozen arguments and discussions around the table.

Like spelling. Stig told them there was a man in England who left a million dollars for anyone who would make spelling sensible.

"Take the word *enough*," Stig said indignantly. "How can anyone make sense of a word like that? Should be *e-n-u-f*. Made me tear my hair out when I was learning English."

Bo was learning to read easily, which Jack said was a relief, considering that she wouldn't read the books Calvert sent. And Graf seemed to have been born reading.

All in all, she and Graf liked school a lot after they'd seen to it that they didn't have to do all the things Calvert told them to.

And so did everyone else at their school, Charlie Hootch and Frenchie, Glenner and Dago Charlie.

Arvid said it was amazing how fast grown-ups learned when they got a chance. Dago Charlie, for instance, learned all the math that he'd have learned in five years of school in just two months.

They learned so fast Arvid said maybe it would be a good idea just to teach everybody when they were grown up instead of wasting eight years or so at it when they were kids and could be having a good time instead of being stuck in school.

Bo said she liked to do school now, while she was little. But Arvid looked grim.

"That's because you don't know nothing about how they do real school. Can't talk, can't move, get your hand smacked or worse if you can't recite your lessons. Big board for paddling. Prison. I hated every minute of it."

So Bo knew she and Graf were very lucky.

CHAPTER TWENTY-SIX

EIGHT CHARLIES

ONE DAY IN EARLY WINTER, they were almost finished with school. Bo had put away her workbooks, and Graf was putting all the crayons in the can. Glenner Campbell had finished all the writing exercises that Stig and Carmen had set for him and was feeling pleased with himself. The rest were leaning back in their chairs, ready for another cup of coffee, when a terrible noise shook the ground.

Everybody around the table looked at one another, suddenly tense.

"Dynamite," they all said.

"Sounded like Donal Sather's direction," Dago Charlie said.

"Probably getting rid of a big stump or some such," Stig said calmly.

"Yeah, most likely," Frenchie agreed uncertainly.

Still they sat tense, listening. Glenner got up and pulled on his parka. "I'll see if anyone knows something," he said.

It wasn't long before Glenner came running back to tell them it was at Donal's mine, and it was terrible.

Cherokee Charlie had been carrying dynamite. He'd tripped, and the dynamite had blown him up.

The men got up and left, all gone to see what they could do.

ALL THE JOKES everyone had made about the nine Charlies seemed sad now. Only eight Charlies left.

They buried him at the graveyard with his headband and his feather that he wore for the Fourth of July. Donal Sather made a speech over the grave about what a good guy Charlie had been. They didn't know who his family was or where they lived. Didn't know who to tell that he was gone.

That night when Graf was already asleep and Jack was tucking Bo in, she asked, "How come they didn't know anything about Cherokee Charlie?"

Jack sat on the chair by her bed and looked down at his hands.

Then he said, "Lot of men come here from other places. Don't tell about nothing, just like they want to forget it," he said.

He was quiet for a minute. "I'm betting Charlie was happy here. He could have gone somewhere else anytime, but he stayed here. Been here a long time. So I figure this was his home, and the boys were his family."

"Like it was at Ballard," Bo said.

"Like it was at Ballard," said Jack.

CHAPTER TWENTY-SEVEN

THE PIANO BOX

BO AND GRAF wished they'd see the Yup'ik boy again, but they never did, not for the rest of that winter. Nita was disappointed, too. He hadn't come to see her for quite a while, but probably he didn't have the right clothes for such a long walk in the winter—ten miles. But at least he had his new warm mukluks. She was glad about that.

Hardy said the men from the Willard dredge were uneasy about him.

They said he didn't ever seem to be with his father, just cut wood for the stove in the cookshack and the bunkhouse. He usually slept in the cook-shack, but sometimes last summer, he had slept in a corner of the dredge. (Bo and Graf made faces when Hardy said that. Imagine sleeping in the dredge.) Nice kid, they said, but he wouldn't talk to them. They figured he was afraid of his father, who was a surly guy. Didn't talk much himself.

There were lots of days when the men at the dredge didn't see Renzo at all.

One bright sunny day in the middle of April, Graf was off by himself, across the tailings, almost up to the hills. The snow had mostly gone, just a little left in the spaces between big rocks.

School was over for the day. Bo had gone to see the horses, Arvid was working at the dredge, and Jack was asleep because he'd been up half the night doing some welding for Hardy.

Even now that Graf was five, he still wasn't sup-posed to go that far away with-out Bo or Buddy or Will. But he had been following a gray vole. They never saw animals around Iditarod Creek—nothing for animals to eat—but there

the vole was. It was almost as if the vole wanted him to follow, the way he'd scamper off and then sit down and watch Graf stumbling across the tailings.

Graf had just decided to turn back when way behind Eller's house, at the edge of the tailing piles, down in a shallow pit, he saw the piano box. The big box they'd shipped Miz Eller's piano in last summer.

Graf knelt at the edge of the tailings and looked down at the box for a long time. It was tipped on its side. The top of the box had been crowbarred off to get the piano out, and that top was propped up to cover the front opening. Like a door.

In front of the box, there was a ring of rocks, and inside the ring were sticks blackened from a fire. There was a little pile of dead spruce branches and twigs nearby, ready for another fire.

A big rock from the tailings was set near the ring of rocks. A place to sit when the fire was burning.

Graf suddenly knew that the Yup'ik boy was living in the piano box. He got to his feet and made his way down the side of the tailings.

He walked quietly around to the front of the box. Graf bent to peek through the opening.

Renzo was inside. He was lying curled up in a

pile of dried grass and was half covered with grass as well. He was wearing a parka, the hood mostly covering his face, and there was a shabby blanket over the parka.

Winter was over, but it was still cold at night, freezing sometimes, and this box couldn't keep anyone warm. Graf had a dread of being cold.

Renzo's eyes suddenly flew open. They looked at each other, both of them horrified.

"Come with me," said Graf. "It's too cold here."

Renzo shook his head wearily and closed his eyes again. He snuffled, and his breathing sounded ragged. Graf was sure he was sick.

Graf straightened up and thought for a minute, then he quietly turned and blundered his way across the tailings, trying hard not to make any noise. When he got to the place where the tailings were packed harder, he started to run.

He ran all the way home and burst into the quiet house. Jack was still asleep.

Graf shook him by the shoulder, and Jack snorted and coughed, then turned over with a groan. Graf shook him again. Jack opened his eyes and focused, then scowled fiercely. "What's wrong?"

"Renzo," said Graf. "He's sick." Jack sat up, puzzled, waiting for the explanation.

"He's living in the piano box."

"Piano box?"

"The one Miz Eller's piano came in."

"Where's it at?" asked Jack, looking a lot smarter now.

"Way behind the Ellers'. He's sick. He wouldn't come with me."

"How do you know he's sick?" asked Jack, pulling on his socks.

"I just do," said Graf.

Jack looked hard at him.

"Never saw you get anything wrong yet," he said and began to lace up his boots.

"We have to bring him here," said Graf.

"I figured that's what you had in mind," said Jack.

Jack picked up Graf to save time and carried him to the piano box, half running, Graf telling him which way to go. Graf told him to be quiet when they got near.

"You think he's going to run?" asked Jack.

Graf just bit his lip. He didn't know.

Jack took in the dead fire and the pile of spruce twigs. He slid the box front away to look at Renzo still sleeping. Saw his tattered blanket, the parka, the piles of dead grass. Saw a half-empty box of crackers in the corner. When he pulled the blanket away, they could see Renzo's face in the bright sunlight, dirty and thin.

Jack bent down and picked him up with one scoop, his skinny legs dangling down, and when Renzo stiffened and cried out, Jack rumbled, "Hush. You're coming with us."

Renzo put his head down and buried his face in Jack's coat. Graf was feeling better now. Jack was like a big stove.

Renzo would be warm now.

CHAPTER TWENTY-EIGHT

BRUISES

BO WAS BACK from the horse barn, sitting on the front step in the spring sun, eating one of the last biscuits from breakfast. She took one look at Graf and what Jack was carrying, and she darted to open the door for them.

"Get the bathtub," Jack ordered. Bo dashed to the back of the house, lifted the tub off its nail, and dragged it into the kitchen. Jack laid Renzo on the couch and waited a moment to see if he would stay put. Jack bobbed his head at Renzo to tell Bo and

Graf that they should watch him. Then he filled the long tub with hot water from the stove.

"Get two big towels from the shelf," he said, "and wait in your room. Boy might want some privacy."

Bo and Graf peeked through their bedroom curtain as Jack put Renzo in the long tub and soaped him from hair to toes, talking gently.

Bo and Graf couldn't hear what Jack was saying; they could only hear the low rumble of his voice. Jack lifted Renzo out of the tub and stood him up to dry him. Impossibly thin legs, ribs standing out. He was a rainbow of bruises. Yellow and green and purple everywhere.

Jack pulled his big flannel shirt off and wrapped it around Renzo. Then he carried him to Arvid's rumpled bed and pulled up the covers. Renzo closed his eyes again after one wild look at Jack.

"Go get Carmen," Jack told Graf.

Then he told Bo to get Eero and Stig. When they came back with Bo, Jack pulled back the shirt to show them the bruises.

"Some old ones, some new ones," said Stig after a minute. "He never got these the usual kid way."

"Back and front," said Jack. "Legs too," he said, showing them the spindly legs, colored all over.

"How'd those boys at the mine let his old man get away with this?" Stig asked, his voice tight.

"Looks like he was too smart to put marks on the kid's face," said Eero.

Renzo kept his eyes closed, his face expressionless and tired.

"Marshal's still in town," Eero said. "I'll get him."

Graf slipped quietly in the door, breathing hard from running. "Carmen says she'll be right up," he whispered.

Jack gave Bo some money. "You and Graf go get some clothes for the kid. Tell Sidney what you need them for; he'll figure it out."

Bo and Graf got back with a bundle Sidney had thrown together—some way too big undershirts and shorts, a pair of wool socks, and a striped miner's shirt.

Carmen came. She looked hard at Renzo, his black curls still wet and his face shiny from the soap, and laid her ear on Renzo's chest. Renzo's startled eyes snapped open, but he didn't pull away.

Carmen looked up at all the faces in the bedroom
doorway.

"Maybe just a bad cold." Bo didn't think Carmen
sounded very certain. "His lungs don't sound too
bad, not like pneumonia or anything. But mercy,
when do you think he ate last?"

"Crackers," said Jack. "That's all he had in the box. Crackers."

Carmen nodded at one of Renzo's skinny arms. "Looks to me like this arm's been broken."

"God almighty," Jack groaned. "I carried him like that with a broken arm?"

"No, no," she soothed him. "Old break, I think. See how it's sticking out here, like it didn't knit together right?"

Bo was sure everyone in the room was thinking the same thing about how Renzo's arm had been broken.

Eero and the marshal came, looking stern. And Arvid was right behind them, mouth in a tight line, so Bo knew he'd been told about Renzo.

When the marshal had looked at Renzo's bruises and his arm, he asked, "Who did this to you?"

Renzo looked down at his bruises as if he hadn't noticed them before. The marshal waited stubbornly, his jaw jutting out to show he wasn't going to stand for any nonsense. There was a long silence, everyone waiting.

"I fell down," said Renzo softly.

WHEN THE MARSHAL was leaving, he told Jack and Eero and Stig that kids who are hurt by their parents usually won't tell on them.

"Most pitiful thing you'll ever see, kid battered, broken bones, say, 'Oh no, my mom never meant to hurt me. It was an accident.' Or 'I'm just clumsy.'" He opened the door. "I'm going out to Willard's to get his old man now."

"Well, if he tries to take the kid, it ain't going to happen," said Jack grimly.

LATER, THE MARSHAL came to tell them what he'd found out at Willard Dredge. Arvid shooed Bo and Graf away. "Don't want the kids to hear this," he said.

But Bo and Graf listened anyway.

The men at the Willard dredge were shocked when the marshal told them about the kid.

"Donatelli's been gone for almost a week. He got his last pay for his winter work and just disappeared. They weren't surprised because they'd been getting on him about the way the boy was neglected. They figured he left the country and took the kid with him. Never dreamed the kid took off on his own. And they never knew the kid was beaten, or they would have done something."

The marshal spent two days with Sherwin at the wireless shack sending wires to Bethel and Fairbanks to see if Donatelli had left Iditarod Creek on any of the planes that had landed in the last few weeks. They tracked him to Fairbanks.

"What I figure is he got worried when the boys at the mine were getting worked up about the way the kid was treated. Cook especially. Bet he's left the country. Bet he's on one of them freighters out of Valdez or Seward."

"Can you find out if he's gone?" asked Arvid.

"Maybe," said the marshal. "Take some time, and depends on if he's using his real name. I'll see what I can see."

CHAPTER TWENTY-NINE

QUIET

RENZO GOT A LITTLE STRONGER every day, but Jack kept him in bed most of the time. He borrowed another cot from Hardy's endless supply and set it up in Bo and Graf's room, crossways at the foot of Graf's bed.

Renzo's breathing was better, and he didn't cough so much.

But he slept a lot. Every time he woke up, Jack would bring him something to eat, and every day Renzo ate more than he had the time before.

A few boys from the Willard dredge visited, joked with him, brought him things—a new pocket knife that made him smile, a harmonica. Nita came too, softly talking to him in Yup'ik.

But still Renzo was quiet, didn't say much except to Bo and Graf when they were alone. It was worrisome how removed he was.

And he would go poker-faced sometimes, especially if one of the boys said something kindly meant. He just didn't seem to know how to handle a thing like that.

"Way I figure it," Jack told the boys, "is he's afraid he's going to cry. You know how it is, you're feeling miserable, but you got it in hand, you're holding up. Then someone says a kind word, and you lose it. Worst thing in the world when you're troubled, sympathy."

Everyone nodded. They all knew how that was.

Arvid sent away for jackets and boots and socks, shirts, Levi's, and underwear. When they came on the mail plane, Jack organized Renzo's clothes—new jacket and three pairs of jeans on the hooks, a sweater, two shirts, underwear, and socks neatly folded on the shelf over Renzo's cot.

Then he patted the stacks of new clothes with satisfaction.

"That's better," Jack said. "You can get dressed and go outside some now. Not for very long. And you got to wear this wool sweater or the jacket and a hat. Not summer yet, and there's not enough meat on your bones to keep you warm."

"I NEVER HAD but two pairs of pants in my life," Renzo told Bo that night. "Didn't know you could have more."

"When we got Graf, he only had one pair," Bo remembered. "And me, I only had one diaper!"

"Your pa's big on clothes, ain't he?" Renzo said.

"It's just he wants everyone to be clean," she said. "Sometimes he'll make me change in the middle of the day." She made her voice go all Southern and slurry and put her hands on her hips the way Jack did. "Child, get out of that sorry mess and change your pants! I think you attracts dirt like honey brings flies!"

Renzo barked his first laugh since he'd been with them.

"Well, he made me take off my shirt so he could sew a button on," he told her, looking amazed.

Bo was sure that it had been a long time since anyone had ever bothered about Renzo's buttons or whether his clothes were clean.

AFTER THEY'D FINISHED lunch one day, Jack got up and put on his work gloves. Time to split wood.

Renzo looked up at him and said quietly, "I could do the wood now."

Jack looked startled. He circled his chin with his thumb and forefinger while he thought, looking at Renzo with narrowed eyes.

Then he said, "You look pretty skookum now. I'd say that's an offer I can't refuse." Jack tossed him the gloves, and Renzo's face lit up.

After Renzo went out the door, Bo and Arvid and Graf looked at Jack reproachfully.

"Way I figure," said Jack, "he don't like to feel useless. If we let him work like the rest of us, he'll feel more at home."

It seemed to be the right thing to do. When Bo and Graf went to bring the split wood in to the wood box, they could see Renzo was happy to be working, his ax high on every upstroke. It didn't seem to tire him at all.

When the marshal wired news about Renzo's father, Jack and Arvid told him at the dinner table.

"Marshal says your father left Alaska last month, boat out of Seward," Arvid said. "I'd say he's not coming back. What do you think?"

Renzo just looked solemn and shook his head. He didn't know.

"Did he tell you he was leaving?"

"I could tell."

"You went to the piano box before he left?"

Renzo gave a short nod, yes.

"Why'd you take off like that?"

Renzo stared at Arvid. Then he said, "I didn't want to go with him."

"I guess not," said Jack, looking dangerous.

ARVID AND JACK eased Renzo into the bunch that came in the morning for school.

Eero started him on the alphabet, and soon everyone was helping him with his reading and arithmetic. He was like Graf—he'd learned to read labels and signs early. It wouldn't take much to teach him the rest.

Renzo was clearly astounded at the talk around the table. He would look from face to face, searching, not sure how to take the jokes and teasing and complaints.

At night, after they were in bed, Bo and Graf and Renzo whispered until one of the papas bellowed at them to go to sleep.

"Don't want to be dragging you three out of bed in the morning!" Arvid said.

Bo told him her story and then she told Graf's story, and she told him so much about all the people in Ballard that he said wistfully, "I wish I could see them."

But he never told them his story.

CHAPTER THIRTY

ANOTHER BOY

ONE NIGHT JACK was going off to the hotel to fix the draft on Hardy's big woodstove.

Bo handed Jack his work gloves, and Jack stuffed them in his pocket. Then he looked straight at Arvid with his two-dimple smile.

"Well?" he said.

Arvid didn't ask "Well what?" He raked his thick fingers through the straight yellow hair over his forehead, all the way to the back where his bald spot was growing, and looked fierce.

"Soon as I saw him, I knew he was going to be number three," Arvid growled. "Hell, I think I knew it first time the kids talked about him. Got a sixth sense about it after these first two we picked up."

Bo beamed. They were talking about Renzo!

Jack put his big hand on Bo's head. "And you be quiet," he said. "Let me and Arvid handle this, you hear? Can't come straight at Renzo with anything. Got to go at it sideways."

Bo nodded happily.

Jack and Arvid both burst into huge rollicking laughs at the same time. "Three kids," muttered Arvid. "*Three.*"

"Don't you say an ever-lovin' word," Jack warned Bo.

THE NEXT MORNING at breakfast, before Arvid went off to do his welding, Jack puttered around the kitchen as usual, humming. Bo and Graf and Renzo were already eating, and Arvid was putting wood in the stove.

Jack put a plate of bacon on the table and said,

casually as could be, "Bo? What do you reckon we should do with Renzo, here?"

Bo looked shocked, and so did Graf and Renzo. But she didn't miss a beat.

"He has to stay with us, Papa. We have to keep him. You know that."

"Just what me and the Swede was saying," said Jack. "What've you got to say, Graf?"

"I'm the one who found him," said Graf, crabby, illogically.

Renzo stood up so suddenly he knocked the chair over. Then he just slipped out the back door and disappeared.

Bo and Graf were worried.

"He didn't even have his boots on," Bo fretted.

But Jack told them, "Leave him be. He'll be back. You know he's not good with feelings."

RENZO CAME BACK at suppertime, slipping in the back door as quietly as he'd left. Jack and Arvid were finishing off a big pot of beans and cornbread, and Bo and Graf were just starting the dishes.

Arvid got up, took Renzo's plate of food out of

the warming oven, and set it on the table. Renzo sat down looking a little shamefaced. But he picked up his fork and started on the food, hardly taking a breath between bites.

"Well, now that you've taken a vacation and thought it over, I take it that you came back to say yes," said Arvid, laughing.

Renzo studied the beans and cornbread on his plate, and then he looked up at them for a second, gave a short manly nod, and began eating again.

Bo and Graf and the papas smiled at one another, their eyes happy.

"Our family just got bigger," said Arvid, as if he was talking about the weather.

"True, true," said Jack just as calmly. "Got ourself another boy."

They knew better than to make a big fuss. If there was anything Renzo could not deal with, it was fuss. They'd learned that much.

CHAPTER THIRTY-ONE

BACK TO WORK

THE ICE WAS MELTING off the dredge ponds, and the mining season was about to start up again. All the men who had gone Outside to spend their money and see their families came back.

They told about the hard times they'd seen Outside. That was called the Depression. Everywhere people had no jobs, and in the cities, people stood in lines to get something to eat at the soup kitchens.

"I tell you boys," Zeke said, "we're lucky to have jobs." They all agreed with him. Even if they wished they didn't have to work around the noisy dredge, they would keep on because some of them had family out of work. They had to send money.

Still, they had wonderful stories to tell about the world out there: the new music they'd heard, the movies called talkies they'd been to, the flying demonstrations, barnstormers with an idiot riding on the wings, the plane that went around the world in eight days. The World Series. Babe Ruth. Will Rogers.

They brought Bo and Graf presents—jigsaw puzzles, jump ropes, jacks, and new records. "Keep Your Sunny Side Up!" "If You Knew Susie." Bo played her favorite—"Ain't We Got Fun?"—so many times Arvid begged for mercy. "Not again," he'd groan, so Bo only played it when he was not in the house.

Best of all was Cracker Jack. Delicious popcorn with caramel and peanuts. There were surprises in the box—tin whistles and little cars and all sorts of things. Bo and Graf wanted to open all the boxes of Cracker Jack at once to get the prizes right away, but Arvid said not to be greedy, and he put them up on the high shelf to dole out one at a time.

The boys were all pleased about Renzo, laughed and joked with him the way they did with everyone.

"Good thing to have a big skookum boy in the family," said Charlie One-Eye. "Can't get any work out of babies for a long, long time."

"I know all about babies," said Jack. "Mama Nancy raised a whole passel of them in her kitchen, including me. And what I know is, you don't want to be trusting babies. Babies is treacherous. All cute and everything, but might turn out to be a pain in the keester. You can't tell what they're like till they're older. After you wasted all that time on them. Babies is a gamble."

"That's true," Arvid agreed, winking at Bo. "Damned dangerous, taking on babies."

CHAPTER THIRTY-TWO

EERO AND STIG

THE DAY BEFORE WORK started on the dredges, Eero and Stig came to the house to talk to Arvid and Jack. They came late, after Bo and Graf and Renzo were in bed, a time they'd never visited before.

Graf and Renzo were asleep, but Bo wasn't. She peeked out of the curtain over their bedroom door and saw Stig unfold a yellow quadrangle map and spread it out on the table.

Jack darted his head at the map. "What's this about?"

Stig pulled a bottle of Charlie's hootch out of his pocket, and Eero brought in a jug of homemade beer.

Arvid laughed at Jack. "God almighty, they mean to talk some serious business here."

Stig and Eero had some mining claims near Ruby, a village on the Yukon. Mammoth Creek. Eero showed Jack and Arvid on the map where the claims were.

"Got these from an old Finn we knew back in the old country. They're patented, so when he died, he left them to us. We never got around to working them." Eero and Stig looked at Jack and Arvid. "We'd like to turn them over to you, pass them along."

Arvid and Jack sent wondering looks at each other, frowning.

"Only thirty feet to clear to get down to bedrock," said Stig. "Got a good house, lots of outbuildings for a shop and suchlike." Stig pointed to another place on the map. "Got Long City here, you know, some roadhouses, few saloons. And lots of good times in Ruby besides." He pointed to another place. "Got a road to Ruby—thirty miles, get your things on the barge in the summer. Best people in the world mining out there."

Eero looked at the papas and beamed. "No more dredge noise! Course, you'd need some equipment, Cat, dragline maybe."

Jack and Arvid shot a worried look at each other. Equipment was expensive. "Don't worry," Eero said, "lots of used machinery around, and that's going to be your main expense. Fuel too, of course. Good mechanics like you, no trouble taking care of your equipment."

"You're *giving* this away," Jack said, unbelieving.

"Yes," said Stig decidedly. "We don't need much—we got enough to see us out. But what we would like to have is the little cabin sitting on the edge of the claim, if that wouldn't inconvenience you." Stig pointed to a spot on the map, a side creek with no name. "It's right here. We been wanting to get away from the dredges ourselves. Never meant to end up in the middle of tailing piles. But we were lazy. Just seemed like a lot of work to start over again at a new place at our age."

Arvid and Jack were almost expressionless.

Then Jack said, "What kind of house?" so Bo knew he was interested.

Stig made a quick drawing on the back of the

map. "Two-story log cabin. Big. In good shape. Can't remember how it was fixed inside," he said. "Me and Eero was just there for a few days."

Jack and Arvid looked at each other.

"I don't know what to say," Jack said. "We'll talk this over, and all I can say is thank you. It's the handsomest offer I ever did hear tell of. I'm half afraid I'll find out I was just dreaming it."

"Well, here," said Stig. He took some glasses off the shelf, set them on the table, and poured whiskey into them. "We'll drink to you thinking about it. No hurry. It ain't going nowhere."

FIRST CHANCE HE GOT, Jack took some time off from work, grabbed a ride with the mail plane, and went with Stig and Eero to look the claims over. He came back looking bigger than when he went away, Bo thought.

"What's it like, Papa?" she asked.

Of course he told them about the house first.

"Biggest place we've ever been in. Bottom half is big as the cookshack in Ballard. Got room enough for anything." He looked off into space, imagining what he could do with that big space. "Big kitchen, place for a bunch of couches and the gramophone, big woodstove, and maybe could have a carpet on the floor. Big old windows and something beautiful to look at out of every one of them."

He looked around at all of them, beaming. "Tall ceilings! Tall doorways, no more ducking to come into a room. Not one of these little piddly cabins. And upstairs, six rooms! Man who built it boarded his mining crew in the house. So not only six rooms upstairs, but the outhouse has three seats!"

Bo and Graf and Renzo squealed. That was fancy. Three holes!

"And there's enough unworked ground to keep us busy till the next century. This here's where we light. No more moving on," Jack said. "I like the people here in Iditarod just fine, none better. But the sound of that dredge? Mmm-mm-*mmm*. Houses that have to move whenever someone takes a notion? And living in tailing piles without trees and animals just ain't natural."

Eero and Stig laughed at him. "All that's true, miles of pure wilderness and packets of animals in the Ruby country," Stig said. "But you got to admit, we don't have many mosquitoes here in Iditarod

Creek. We promise you'll have more than enough mosquitoes in Mammoth Creek to take an edge off that happiness."

BO AND GRAF were sad to leave everyone, but Arvid showed them on the map how close they'd be. People could easily visit from Iditarod Creek.

"Not a long trip overland at all. No river to cross, so I'd bet you'll see plenty of everyone. Winter and summer. Bit longer by boat, but still. Ben said he'd bring Buddy and Will for sure. Don't forget, we got planes now too. And the mail comes fast. Probably get letters every day!"

And Stig and Eero were going to move to the little cabin as soon as they could.

"We'll gather everyone around us sooner or later," Arvid said. "Tell you what. When Oscar is big enough to do a man's work, we'll send for him, too."

"I hope there's lots of kids around Mammoth Creek," Bo said.

Graf was stacking the dishes to be washed. He was precise about this. All the same size dishes together, all the spoons together, all the knives together. Precise and slow.

"Don't need any other kids," he said to the silver-ware. "There's three of us," he said.

SO WHEN THE MINING at Petrovich's mine was over—after a going-away party at Hardy's hotel—they were back in the poling boat. A little more crowded this time with Renzo.

Down the winding and sluggish Iditarod to the Yukon, and then up the Yukon, running their little motor all the way to Ruby, gramophone on the bow again.

It was late in the fall, just a few yellow leaves on the trees, so there were no mosquitoes and no gnats to drive them crazy.

And it was more fun with Renzo. Every night when they were squished together in their sleeping bags under the bow, they'd talk about what they'd do in Mammoth Creek.

Tundra and birds and flowers and a little creek to wade in. Good fishing for grayling a short walk away.

A place to do their school that wasn't the kitchen table, so their schoolwork wouldn't have to be cleared off for every meal.

And a room for each one of them!

But after they'd thought about that for a while, they all decided that they didn't want to sleep in a room by themselves. How could they talk at night like they always did?

Bo popped her head out from under the bow.

"Papas," she called happily, "just think. If we hadn't run out of gold at Ballard, we wouldn't have gone to Iditarod Creek, and we wouldn't have lived next to Eero and Stig, and we wouldn't have a new mining camp of our very own now.

"And if Miz Eller didn't get a piano, there wouldn't have been a piano box, and if Graf didn't follow that vole, we wouldn't have Renzo!"

Arvid and Jack smiled at each other.

Thinking backwards again, their Bo.

AUTHOR'S NOTE

In Alaska the name *Eskimo* is used, not *Inuit*. Canadian and Greenland Inuits have opted to call themselves *Inuit*, the name of their common language, because the word *Eskimo* had come to be regarded in Canada as pejorative. But two major Eskimo languages are spoken in Alaska, only one of which is Inuit. So the Inupiat and Yup'ik—both members of the Inuit Circumpolar Council—continue to call themselves *Eskimo* because the term is inclusive and has never been controversial in Alaska.

Readers may be disturbed by the use of the word *nigger*. Of course this is an offensive term, but it was a word any child in America would have encountered at that time, or this. My book would be less than honest or historically accurate if I had not included the moment when Bo and Graf first heard the word.

So many people of that period were clueless. Political correctness had not yet been invented. Well-meaning people were quite comfortable casually using flippant, slighting names for people who were looked upon as different or considered not quite mainstream.

Bo and Graf didn't have to encounter toxic racism because it wasn't part of the world I wrote about, but I was glad to confront the mindless labeling that *was* so prevalent.

Made in the USA
Middletown, DE
02 July 2021